SHILLING & FLORIN

BOOK FIVE:
A COLD & BITTER REVENGE

KATE HALEY

For Jesse
You know what you did.

CONTENTS

Visit **www.katehaleyauthor.com** for
deals and current news from the author.

1

The sounds of the keys on the typewriter were the loudest sounds in the darkness. They were frantic. Panicked. They drowned out the heavy, laboured breathing of the typist. They drowned out the rattle of the teacup and saucer, with the little metal spoon clinging on the porcelain, as the bangs of the typewriter shook the rickety desk.

They drowned out the sound of the wind outside and the creaks and thuds of the upstairs neighbours. Those strange and ominous sounds of the middle of the night, when most of the world slept. But now was not the time to sleep. Not with the truth pouring in slow and desperate moans into the world, and the typewriter churning as though possessed — the keys drowning out all other noise.

They even drowned out the ghost at the window.

Morning dawned clear and bright. It was good luck, supposedly. It certainly felt like good luck. Although, Charlie was prepared to admit that every morning for the last few months had felt like good luck. The days were short and dark, but the weather seemed to be ignoring winter as best it could. The icy chill of December hadn't done much more than pleasantly temper the stench of the city, and he was grateful for the lack of snow. Charlie was woken by sunlight streaming through the gap in the curtains. It was soft and warm. There was birdsong outside. All in all, it was a rather pleasant way to wake.

Then it got better. With a stretch and a moan, Amy rolled over beside him and curled up against his shoulder. She clutched at him with drowsy but determined fingers. Her curls were silky against his skin and her lips pressed warmly to his bare shoulder.

"Good morning," he smiled, turning into her and planting a kiss on her brow.

"I'm sleeping," she insisted, nuzzling in against him and making herself comfortable, half-sprawled over his side. She was careful never to climb on him, never to pin him down or trap him, but she was still quite possessive. Charlie rather liked it.

"Are you sure…?" he checked. He rolled into her embrace, slipping down against her to plant another kiss at the corner of her lips. His hands explored her naked body beneath the sheets. She gave a soft, approving moan as his fingers roamed to her liking.

"I could be persuaded to wake…" she reconsidered, turning toward his kiss.

He was prepared to ask what might persuade her, but she silenced his inquiry in a manner that suggested he was already on the right track. Her lips locked with his and her hands clutched him to her, messing his hair. Her breath in his mouth was hot and there was an urgency to it that responded to the ways he touched her. He lay half over her, her legs tangled in his, and moved his hands in accordance with the sounds of her appreciation. She began to whisper his name as he traced his lips down the side of her neck.

A sharp knock on the door interrupted them.

"Go away!" Amy bellowed at the door, clutching Charlie's face possessively to her breast.

"It can't wait!" Henry Pound's voice called back, followed immediately by the turning of the doorhandle.

Charlie burrowed under the blankets instantly. Part of his brain was aware that the action placed him in a position to make things look worse, but his cowardice in the face of Lord Pound in the mornings overruled all else. It stemmed, he thought, from the same strange part of his mind that was — against all logical reason — embarrassed to be caught in someone else's bed.

Lord Pound stomped into the room like a small earthquake and Charlie could feel Amy pull the sheets carefully over her chest as she sat up against him.

"And a rude and intrusive morning to you too, Daddy," she huffed at her father.

"Charles," Pound addressed the lump in his daughter's blankets sternly from the end of the bed. "If you're going to spend your time frolicking in Amelia's sheets, you can have the decency to look me in the eye."

Charlie heard the demand, and he heard good reason in it. He did not feel any burning compulsion to move.

"Leave him alone, Daddy," Amy sighed. "If you need to see him so pressingly, you can wait until we're up."

"This can't wait," Pound repeated.

Charlie could hear the sound of a newspaper being rustled. Curiosity finally overcame trepidation. He slowly edged his nose above the edge of the blankets, and the rest of his head and shoulders followed.

Pound looked like a thundercloud at the end of the bed. He was already fully dressed for the day, but it was probably rather late in the morning… and it had been such a pleasant late morning. The severity of his expression quickly erased Charlie's embarrassment. He looked up at Pound shrewdly, calculating the gravity of the situation.

"What happened?" he asked.

"Another woman from the Houses was killed last night," Pound answered, tossing the paper onto the blankets before them. "And it gets worse."

JACK OF HEARTS STRIKES AGAIN was printed in block letters on the page. Charlie immediately noted Lionel Tanner was the attributed author.

"Again?!" Amy cried, snatching for the paper. "How?! Harry's dead."

But Charlie could see the article even as she snatched it up beside him. He could skim the text. Charles Shilling — the real Jack of Hearts. The ultimate evil criminal mastermind. His own villainous genius is the reason he's so good at catching other criminals. Shilling is the real Jack of Hearts and he had Harry framed and murdered.

"Well..." Charlie breathed softly. "This is going to be an interesting morning..."

"It gets worse," Pound repeated.

"It gets worse than another woman brutally murdered and Lionel telling everyone it was me?" Charlie replied.

"It says 'anonymous source'," Amy muttered from where she was reading.

"That just means he made it up and no one can prove he didn't," Charlie grated. "It won't stick. They investigated me, remember? When the Jack's murders began, and I was trying to help, but the police decided that I was a local maniac and likely suspect. I have sound alibis for too many of the murders. Your people have already proven I didn't do this."

"Charlie..." Amy murmured. "It gets worse..."

Charlie rolled his eyes.

"This article claims you killed Kopeck." Amy's nose wrinkled distastefully. "Ugh, he ties his claims to eugenics... that's disgusting. Still, it's a problem, Charlie. If Tanner can provide any evidence against you for Kopeck... more people will start to believe him about the Jack too."

"Or the reverse..." Charlie mused. "Perhaps, if we can absolutely prove I'm not the Jack, it will shift suspicion from Kopeck."

"Charles," Pound began again.

"I know, it gets worse!" Charlie huffed, mussing his hair in frustration. "How, Henry? How does it keep getting worse? Are there two dead women?"

"God save us, I hope not," Pound sighed. "But the

police let me know about the crime before the early edition came through. They found the body last night at 3am. Exactly the same. Coroner thinks the same weapon was used. They checked evidence. The knife they took when they arrested Harry — the knife everyone was certain was the murder weapon — has gone missing. No one knows when it disappeared or how long it's been gone."

Charlie stared at him. He could feel Amy freeze at his side. They were both looking at Henry. They were almost certainly all thinking the same thing. Charlie said a very bad word. No one disagreed.

"The only other piece of evidence missing from the case is the journal," Pound continued softly. "You still have it, don't you?"

Charlie waited a moment, but reality didn't go away or become any easier to deal with, so he began to nod slowly. Amy also said a very bad word. General consensus understood how bad the situation looked. Still, Amy could alibi him for last night. At least he had that. The real problem was going to be solving the case when everyone in London believed he was the culprit. How was he going to find out who killed that woman, and protect any future victims, if no one trusted him? Well, there clearly wasn't 'no one' who trusted him. Amy was still beside him, Pound was warning him, and no one had shown up to detain him this morning. That meant something. Even if all it meant was Pound was putting his foot down right now.

"We need to fix this," Charlie muttered, throwing back the blankets and climbing from the bed. Propriety had not occurred to him until Pound turned around very sharply. His Lordship stayed facing away as Charlie and Amy scrambled from the bed and dressed hurriedly.

"Tanner or the mortician first?" Amy asked, pulling on her dress and adjusting the laces.

"The police wish to speak with you at the morgue, Charles," Pound informed them politely, before Charlie could answer. "Once you are suitably clothed."

"Then we swing by them first," Charlie muttered. "We can see the body and confirm as much of this for ourselves as possible. But quickly. Afterwards, I'm going to shake Lionel down so hard his brains rattle."

"Amelia—" Pound began.

"You can't make this personal, Charlie," Amy warned, ignoring her father. "I know he started it, I know it is, but you can't rise to the bait. It will only make it worse."

"I'm not trying to," Charlie answered, buttoning his shirt. "Lionel is the most interesting piece of this puzzle. The state of his story implies he could even have known about the murder before it happened. I need to know everything he knows. Also, with the libel case ongoing, it was an unbelievably bold or stupid decision to publish that story. Either he has been severely duped into believing this nonsense is somehow real, or someone is forcing him to do this to further their agenda."

"You think that's likely?" Amy grimaced. Charlie joined her to help her finish lacing her dress.

"I can only speak for what I know," Charlie

muttered, his fingers nimbly tying off her bodice ribbons. "I know that a woman is dead. I know that she was killed in a manner that copycatted a known serial killer — possibly even with the same weapon stolen from evidence. I know I didn't do it but that I've been accused of it. I also know that it is not in my accuser's nature to commit such a crime. But someone did, and somehow Lionel found out about it."

"You're right," Amy sighed, adjusting her corsetry. "Tanner wouldn't kill anyone. Not even for a story. He might be malicious, but he's a coward, not an idiot. Someone got to him, and it could even be the killer."

"So, Lionel is a person of considerable interest," Charlie agreed, slinging his coat on. "I will be seeing him the instant I have confirmed the body of this copycat victim for myself."

"Don't you have somewhere else to be?" Pound reminded his daughter pointedly, as they strode either side of him towards the door.

Amy froze and swore again. Charlie paused and blinked slowly. Of course, he had entertained the superstitious notion that sunshine this morning was lucky. The wedding. He turned slowly to look at Amy.

"I can deal with this," he told her. "You have to go play Maid of Honour."

"No." Amy shook her head, to his surprise. "Give me a minute and I'll pen them a letter. Someone can drop it off. I—" her voice caught as she faced him and he realised he was giving her a look. "Charlie, a woman died. Somehow, by some nightmare, it's connected to Harry. Someone imitating the Jack has to be. That… that is more important. I know it's rude, but it just is. Jane and Laura will understand. I know them. They're my best friends. They will understand."

Charlie didn't argue. If Amy believed that, then he trusted her. Besides, they were already hours behind the ball on this one. He could spare a few minutes for her to pen a note to her friends.

2

The day was too beautiful for disaster, and yet disaster had struck. Sunshine did not stave off tragedy. Decorations and carollers lining the street on the way here felt like a sick farce, like an entirely different world to the one she lived in. Amy was painfully nauseated with guilt. She wasn't sure if she felt more guilty for the death of the woman in the paper or skipping out on her Maid of Honour duties. One of those she carried a lot more fault for, but the other felt more harrowing.

The Jack of Hearts murders had always bothered her, not just on an empathetic, personal level, but as a distressed citizen. They were some of the most disturbing and heinous crimes she had ever heard of, let alone witnessed. She had been determined to bring the killer to justice. When she had found out it was Harry… everything changed. The devastation was irreparable, not just to her family and their reputation, but to her heart. It wasn't the obvious betrayal, confusion, and heartbreak. No. It was the guilt. It was the guilt that if she had never existed, those women might never have died.

Now there was a new one, and the guilt was fresh and raw all over again. It could not have come at a worse time. Hopefully, she would be able to keep her feelings in check, and she was grateful she had Charlie's hand to hold — grateful that he'd hold her hand in public now. The only thing worse than the guilt was the anger. She clung to Charlie like she could somehow undo what Tanner had done to him, but that was impossible. Between the guilt and the fury, her blood was so chilled she felt almost numb.

Amy was surprised, almost pleased, when the officers that met them at the morgue turned out to be Wilson and Bond. Charlie's expression was not overwhelmed with confidence when he saw them, but if he was concerned, he managed to keep a lid on it.

"I think I've asked this before, but why is it always you two?" he asked.

"Yep," Wilson gave him a look, "was just saying the same thing to Bond."

"Presumably there is an official investigation launched," Charlie commented. "Aren't you two overstepping your bounds?"

"Detective Rupee is heading the case. She asked us to manage you," Wilson replied. "Might be news to you, Shilling, but the law wasn't overly fond of you before you got your name in the papers."

Amy gave Charlie a warning look to stand down, and she noticed Bond do the same thing to Wilson. The ladies were on duty to keep their partners in check.

"We know you didn't do it, Shilling," Bond assured. "That's why we wanted to see you."

"Hmph," Wilson made a noise that managed to both agree and disapprove at the same time. "Talked to the mortician. They're not happy, but we want your opinion on this. Something ain't sitting right."

"We know you'd be able to spot it," Bond admitted.

"Happy to help," Charlie replied. "I want this killer behind bars before they can hurt anyone else."

"I thought you didn't believe in prison," Wilson quipped as he held the door open for them.

"You think I despise incarceration?" Charlie replied. "Wait 'til you see how I feel about psychopathic killers."

"As opposed to regular killers…?" Bond asked in confusion, following them inside.

"Let's just say if the person on the slab was this woman's attacker, and she'd gutted them instead, I'd have a lot more patience for the killing," Charlie grated.

Amy held his hand tighter. She knew what he meant. She knew how he felt. She hoped the squeeze was reassuring and took the reciprocal touch as confirmation. He had told her on the way over that he wanted nothing more than to find out this was some lovers' quarrel. That the poor woman had been slain by a girlfriend she was breaking up with, and that her killer had panicked and staged something hideous to throw suspicion off her. But he'd also admitted he didn't believe it. He'd been the first one to hypothesise that the original Jack might have been a woman, but that was back when he'd run out of male suspects. They both knew the truth. The ability to butcher a woman like that took strength and misogyny. Or intense hatred. To hack open a person like cattle was not a feat performed lightly.

It was cold and dark in the morgue after the bright

merriments of outside. Amy missed the sun instantly. She missed the songs and the festivities and anything that made her feel like she could belong to a world that wasn't this one. She shouldn't be here. She should be out in the garden making sure the wedding preparations were coming along and making sure Jane was all right. Instead, here she was, investigating a dead woman on a slab.

Bond and Wilson escorted them inside, and Amy was strangely grateful for their company. Until she saw Bond giving her a strange side-eye. She knew what it was before the constable said anything, and the resignation had already set in.

"I don't know if it's your kind of thing, Doctor Florin…" she began, "but there's this book I think you'd really—"

Amy shook her head and tried not to look like she wanted to turn on her heel and run. Something must have betrayed her, because Wilson elbowed Bond knowingly and she shut up.

"Yup. Not the time," she agreed bashfully.

Amy didn't trust herself to say anything. It was most definitely not the time. A sentiment that was reinforced as soon as she saw the girl on the table. She didn't recognise her, which she took as a great mercy, but she immediately felt her heart break. The lady was probably near her in age, but she seemed so much younger. Her skin was icy white and her face smooth and expressionless with death. It made her look almost childlike.

"Oh, you were not wrong…" Charlie whispered,

letting go of Amy and approaching the body. "This is all off…"

Amy stood frozen by the door for a moment as Charlie began his investigation. She knew this was her moment, her time to step up, but she didn't want to get closer to this girl or the absolute horror that had befallen her. She could almost feel it… being back in her room, seeing Harry's wounds for the first time… *knowing*… her breath tightening…

"It looks the same," Bond commented. "And the coroner says it is the same, so what is it that's off?"

Charlie had donned gloves. He barely inspected the wounds, but instead lifted the eyelids to check the body's eyes.

"Everything's wrong…" he muttered. "She bears no resemblance to the others."

"Whadaya mean?" Wilson demanded. "She's a High House lady, ain't she?"

Charlie looked up with the most scathing expression possible on his crooked face. His woeful frustration was quite ready to take the officer to school on the variation of physical human anatomy, but the expression quickly slipped away before he said anything and was replaced with concern.

"Florin, are you all right?" he asked.

Amy nodded and got a grip on herself, steadying her emotions. He still called her by her surname when they were in professional situations. She came forward and donned her own gloves, keeping her eyes on the task at hand and avoiding looking at the body for as long as possible. She skimmed over the notes scrawled on the board beside the slab. Sarah Tuppence. She'd earnt her position. Didn't come from money. And she was one of Bronny's girls. Charlie would be furious.

"Five-nine," Amy commented numbly. "She's quite tall."

"Height always ranged in the original victims," Charlie muttered, sniffing delicately. "But they were all chosen for features that reminded Harry of you — dark skin, or red hair, or green eyes. This lady is blonde, blue eyed, pale — even her shape is dissimilar to yours. She is not nearly as full of figure—" Charlie stopped abruptly, blinking at Amy with those concerned grey eyes she had come to find so endearing. "I'm sorry. I'm making it worse, aren't I?"

"You're doing your job, Charlie," she replied, swallowing uncomfortably. "Everything you've said is true."

"Yes, but..." he muttered apologetically. "You shouldn't be here, Florin... this is... and I'm— I'm doing it again. Rebecca has said I need to try and be more aware of when the truth is painful to others. I'm aware of when it hurts me, I need to try and be conscious of its effect on everyone. This... will be traumatic for you."

"Like it isn't for you?" she smiled sadly at him. "I know you, Charlie. You get distant and hyper-logical when you're repressing. Let's just agree that this is awful and get it done."

Charlie nodded, but the expression in his eyes didn't change. She was glad it didn't. It helped. The way he looked at her, like if she needed him to he would drop the case and elope with her to keep her safe, was the most comforting thing she could imagine. The man across the slab was an undiagnosed genius, even if he was a little mad, and she was going to help him catch whoever had done this and make London safe again.

She steeled herself and began to inspect the wounds. Just like the other women, poor Sarah Tuppence had been stabbed in her neck and bled out, before having her chest cut open and her heart removed. It certainly looked like it could have been done by the same weapon, especially as it had been removed from evidence. Although, she was also certain Harry hadn't been the only man in London with an expensive hunting knife.

There was bruising across her neck and chest where she had been held. Further bruising across her arms. This murder had been more of a struggle than the others and the knife work wasn't nearly as clean. She noticed the written notes did not include those differences. Then she bothered to read the name that signed them off, at the same moment she heard footsteps enter the room.

"You have got to be shitting me!" Monty demanded in outrage.

"Careful, Mont," Wilson warned.

"We need their expertise," Bond added placatingly.

"You let the killer into my morgue!" Monty shouted.

Amy wasn't entirely sure when she had picked up the scalpel, she just knew it was in her hand when she turned, and that she was holding it in a rather violent position. The next thing she knew, Charlie's hand was over hers, gently forcing her to lower the blade, and taking it from her grasp. Monty stood in the doorway, watching them like she'd just caught them in the act of murder.

"Let's all just calm down, okay?" Bond mediated, stepping between them and motioning for a de-escalation. "Come on, Monty. That story was balderdash. We know he didn't do it."

"Lord Pound himself alibied him," Wilson agreed.

"He's tricked them…" Monty hissed. "I knew it. I knew it last time I saw you, Doctor Florin, he's got his claws in. He's tricked you and your father. Don't let him do this."

Amy knew she was angry. She knew she was so angry she could feel her blood chill and her eyes set. She knew the anger showed, but she felt completely calm as she stared Monty down. Amy wasn't well acquainted with the quirky mortician, but she knew the other woman had been a fan of Harry's. Not of his work as the Jack, but of his character at the social clubs they both attended. Monty had refused to believe Harry was the Jack, and Amy didn't blame her. It would be much easier to deny that painful truth. She'd be much happier without it. But it was too obvious to deny. Just like the wounds on poor Sarah behind her…

"How deep in this are you, Monty?" Amy whispered.

She could feel glances of confusion cast her way by everyone, but she ignored them all to hold the mortician's gaze.

"Charlie couldn't have done this," Amy stated. "He

physically couldn't have. He's not tall enough and his arms aren't long enough. Sarah was attacked by someone holding her across the chest from behind, and then stabbing her in the throat from over her shoulder. They were taller than her and they struck down, not up. You're looking for someone over six foot, yet you're standing here pointing fingers and accusing Shilling — who's shorter than either of us. I refuse to believe you are that bad at your job. It's more likely you're an accomplice. So, tell me, how deep in this are you?"

"He could have been standing on a ledge to get that height!" Monty snapped. "You don't get to come in here with that psychopath and start accusing me of—!"

Amy lunged. If Charlie hadn't grabbed her she probably would have attacked Monty. As it was, she dragged him halfway across the room before he dug his heels in.

"Amy!" he exclaimed. "Jesus and Mary…! Amy, stop!"

His voice made her halt before she was able to backhand Monty across the face. It was all she wanted right now. The anger and grief bubbling up made it feel like if she could hit Monty hard enough, she could bring Sarah back. It made no sense, but nothing did right now. The Jack of Hearts was back and nothing made sense. Charlie had called her Amy like things were getting personal. She'd made him promise they wouldn't, and here she was breaking her own rule.

Monty was cowering. She had balked when Amy went for her. The fire behind her rage went out at the sight. Monty might be helping someone target Shilling, but she was far too much of a coward to have shed blood herself. That was the real problem though — the sheer number of people who wanted to throw rocks at Charlie just because he didn't conform. Half of London could be in on it.

"He didn't do this, Monty," Amy insisted, letting Charlie hold her back. His embrace soaked up some of the pain, leaving space to breathe again. "We both know he didn't. Why are you pushing this agenda? Your report is supposed to be analytical. It's supposed to help us catch whoever did this."

"Speaking of," Charlie interrupted, letting go of her to point to evidence on Sarah, "there are distinctive bruises on our victim. I think that there may even have been more than one attacker, or she tried to fight back but the assailant was significantly stronger. See these bruises around the neck? She was choked before she was stabbed. You lose part of the imprint because of the knife wound, which is unfortunate, but it would be worth measuring that mark against the ones on her arms to see if the hands that grabbed her range in size. Also, these bruises on her arms here, this darker imprint suggests that perhaps the attacker is wearing a sizable ring on their middle finger." He held up his hands. "You may take measurements of my hands to match against the body," he offered. "But I didn't do this."

"Monty already has your details on file from the first time," Amy muttered. "She can already prove it wasn't you — if only she felt like getting justice instead of persecuting nonconformists."

"How dare you—" Monty started. Wilson put a

hand on her shoulder and gave her another warning look. Amy took the opportunity to double down.

"You're letting a killer go free, Monty, just so you can take a swipe at Shilling that won't work."

"And you're letting Harry's killer into your bed," Monty snapped. "Which one of us is more deluded?!"

"That's what you think?!" Amy cried. "Then you are! You're certifiably insane! Harry killed himself! And Charlie was in France!"

"Well, isn't that convenient?" Monty snarled.

"It's convenient that I was in France," Charlie agreed. "I think otherwise you and your cronies would have had me formally investigated. However, Harry's death in itself was not overly convenient, no. I will concede that not having to put anyone through a trial over the Jack of Hearts may have been a mercy, but it does leave a certain absence of closure."

"You mean it leaves no one investigating so that the Jack can come back and do this?" Monty snapped.

"The person who did this is not the same killer," Charlie gestured. "They are a copycat, and a rather sloppy one — which you are well aware of, Monty."

He did that thing. Amy was watching him as he did it. She didn't know how he did it, but there was a set to his eyes and a severity in his tone. It was that cadence that always made people pay attention, that got even the nobility that wanted to trounce him to shut up and take notice. He was warning her. Not just that it was a different killer, but that he could prove that she knew.

"It's the same M.O.," Monty grated.

"No," Charlie shook his head. "It's not, and you

know that. All this copies is the attack pattern, which was publicised. Anyone who read a newspaper could have copied this much. All the actual details are wrong."

"There's all the dissimilarities you mentioned before," Amy added. "Coupled with the lack of perfume."

"Indeed, Florin," Charlie smiled at her. "I had yet to mention, but you are quite correct. Harry gave all the original victims the same perfume as a gift beforehand. An expensive perfume — your perfume — that he had them wear presumably when he lay with them and which was obviously still on their person when he slaughtered them—" Charlie cut himself off abruptly and glanced her way, the confidence in his eyes softening. "I'm so sorry…"

Amy closed her eyes and shook her head at him. They'd be here forever if he kept stopping to apologise for wrongs Harry had done. It wasn't his fault, and from the shaken look on Monty's face, she clearly needed to hear about them. The perfume had, after all, been Charlie's discovery. It might have been new information to the morgue and the police.

"When the Jack killed," Charlie began with his usual conviction, overlayed with an obvious discomfort at recounting details in front of Amy, "he did it with care. The women he murdered were killed quickly, so as to limit their suffering, and once dead, their hearts were carefully removed and preserved. They were killed by someone obsessed with them, or at least by someone obsessed with the person they saw in each of them.

Someone who had to possess their hearts completely. There was a reverence in that slaying which becomes all the more obvious looking at the copycat here. This woman completely differs from the standard M.O. — save for her job, again well publicised information — and she was butchered without care, by someone who had no concern for her. There is no intimacy in this killing. There is no reverence. You can tell from the cuts on the ribs and tissue that the heart was probably damaged in removal. I honestly doubt the killer even kept it. They only used this method as homage to the Jack, not because they had any desire or imagination themselves."

Amy knew she should be horrified, and part of her was, but watching him work was such an art. He saw things in death others didn't. He saw the art in crime. That's why other people found him uncomfortable. It wasn't just that he lived according to a different moral code to everyone else, a code which made him appear scruffy and rude to genteel folk, it was that he could see dark hearts, and when he saw them, he looked closer instead of turning away. She had a sneaking suspicion that if questioned, he would perhaps compare the killings to the Renaissance. This new murder was a child's sketch of a Botticelli and, when hung in the same gallery, the differences were painfully obvious. She could imagine the comparison in his voice.

Monty was looking at them a little sickly. She wanted it to be Charlie and, soothed by following his thought process and imagining his mind, Amy could see why Monty wanted it to be Charlie. She didn't have

Charlie's sympathy though. Charlie could empathise and explain. Amy still wanted to hit Monty with a brick until she did her job. She glared at the mortician with absolute venom, and she had the backup of the constables who were also paying rapt attention.

"I'll— I'll make the notes..." Monty muttered, reluctantly picking up the paperwork to avoid all the eyes on her.

"At least we know for sure..." Charlie sighed, peeling off his gloves. "I must admit, when Henry showed me the paper this morning... I almost doubted us, Florin."

Amy looked to him, blinking in surprise.

"Not properly, of course," he admitted. "I know you're a genius, and your work catching the Jack was flawless. I knew you had succeeded everywhere I failed in that case, and I didn't really doubt you, but a tiny part in the back of my mind was terrified I had missed something again. At least now we know for certain this is an entirely separate killing."

"We don't know that," Amy murmured, wanting to be grateful for his faith but falling short. "Someone is trying to copy Harry. That makes it connected."

"We'll see," Charlie grimaced. "God herself knows there are some very ill people out there who admired the Jack, it could be that simple."

Amy nodded. It could be. He was right. He was a genius and it could be everything he said.

It didn't feel that simple.

It felt personal.

Charlie had already made light of the attack on him.

He was acting like he'd brushed it off, like people accused him of murder all the time. She supposed he was very used to it. She wasn't. She wasn't used to watching him be accused. Not during the months she'd been in love with him. This murder had been part of a deliberate attack on his character. It felt very personal. That meant the next person to check with was Charlie's accuser. It was time to have a chat with Lionel Tanner.

3

Lionel Tanner lived in a ground floor apartment in a brick townhouse. There was what would have been a small but quaint garden outside, if it had not become so unruly and overgrown. Ivy was starting to creep up the walls, and the fence was disappearing into the trees and shrubs. There were painted pinecones and baubles strung up in the foliage. Seasonal cheer. Charlie stood and considered it. Meanwhile, Amy knocked on the door to the building and explained, in her best Doctor Florin voice, what the situation was to the landlady, who was suitably impressed with Lord Pound's daughter and let them in immediately.

So far, so painless. Charlie wasn't holding his breath that it would stay that way. He couldn't believe he was thinking it, but he rather wished the police had accompanied them here. They certainly had a way of opening doors that he didn't. Unfortunately, they had already questioned Lionel, decided he was quite mad, and they needed to report on what Shilling and Florin had found at the morgue. Apparently, Charlie had to put his faith in Wilson and Bond for damage control. It really was the end of the world. Of course the world would end at Christmas. Cursed season.

To say that Lionel was not pleased to see them was an understatement. To say that Amy didn't care and was ready to level the man with a shovel was even more so. The look on both their faces as she forced her way into his apartment conjured in Charlie a surprise that Amy wasn't hiding a weapon in her skirts.

"You can't be here!" Lionel screamed, going bug-eyed. "He's a murderer! Doctor Florin, you have to get away from him!"

"He's really not the one you have to be worried about right now, Lionel," Amy warned in a deadly tone.

Charlie had to remind himself silently that Amy wasn't being unreasonable. She was taking the entire ordeal very personally. But then, if their positions had been reversed, he might well have been blind with fury that someone would slander her so. This was not, by a very long way, the first time that Lionel had publicly and falsely accused Charlie of murder. In fact, it was the first time ever that Lionel had accused Charlie of something he'd actually done. Charlie had to admit he was more than a little curious as to how Lionel had found out the truth about Kopeck.

He took in the apartment as they entered. It was a one-room boarding situation, by the look of it, and it was in a state of absolute shambles. But Charlie was used to shambles. He lived in mess himself, when given the choice. It left everything open to the eyes and easy to find. There was order to the chaos. Although, he was prepared to admit he couldn't read the order in this chaos. This looked like madness. Something he was accused of frequently, and therefore slow to judge.

"You have to understand, Doctor," Lionel pleaded, "I know the truth now! I always suspected! But I see it! He told me! You've been tricked, my Lady!"

"Tanner, I wouldn't trust you as far as I could throw you," Amy snapped. "But after the stunt you pulled, you are going to jail. Forget inciting a panic and disturbing the peace, the lawyers will take the libel case to trial. You're done. You might want to start coughing up why you did it."

"Master Pound told me!" Lionel protested.

Charlie stalked slowly through the room. The house had initially been pungent with pine when they entered, which unsurprisingly suggested the landlady had a fresh Christmas tree set up in one of the nearby spaces... but the smell wasn't nearly as strong in Lionel's apartment. He had other scents fighting for dominance, and most importantly, did not leave his door open very often. There was an unmade bed and a messy wardrobe, but they were almost hidden in the jumble of other items. He eyed up the notes of scrawled ramblings everywhere, the old newspapers, Lionel's typewriter on the desk against the back wall... even the man himself.

Lionel was not how Charlie remembered him. The journalist — if he could be called that — was usually just a greased-up slimeball with malicious cunning in his eyes and scandal in his pocket. Right now, the man's eyes were bloodshot, his hair a mess, his clothes dirty and rumpled. He did look quite mad. His condition had given Charlie cause to hesitate in his investigation. This was not someone they could shake sense or guilt from.

That limited their methods of deduction.

"Master Pound?" Amy echoed.

"Pound Junior's ghost!" Lionel wept. "He was here at the window last night! He told me everything!"

Charlie kept his eyes on the man and the room as he picked up the teacup on Lionel's desk and gave it a gentle sniff. That was the notable scent beneath the overwhelming fresh pine.

"Harry's ghost?" Amy repeated. Charlie watched her with soft eyes. There was a gentle patience blossoming in her the longer Lionel talked. He sounded like a madman, and Charlie could see Amy's training kicking in as the understanding that she was dealing with someone having a psychotic break overruled her anger. They both had every reason not to like Lionel, but the man's distress was very real.

"Don't touch that!" Lionel screamed at Charlie, motioning frantically to him like he was swatting a bug. "Don't touch my things! You'll poison me! You'll kill me! Murderer!"

"You've already been drugged, Lionel," Charlie sighed. "Though by guile or choice, I have yet to determine." Charlie held the cup out to Amy. "Smell this."

Amy sniffed the cup delicately and frowned. "It's too earthy to just be tea…" she commented.

"Quite," Charlie agreed, swapping for the teapot and removing the lid to sniff. The scent was stronger than he remembered and he pulled a surprised face. Amy gave it a delicate sniff, although the scent carried.

"Mushrooms?" she exclaimed softly. "Why?"

"You poisoned me!" Lionel shrieked, grabbing a blanket from his unmade bed and pulling it over his head, screaming into the fabric.

"A better question would be 'why not?'," Charlie supplied. "I've tried this species before, they're quite popular psychedelics, although..." he gave the screaming Lionel a look, "paranoia is a common side effect."

"You've tried them?" Amy queried, with rather more judgement than Charlie thought necessary.

"I was injured and Rebecca insisted I stay in bed for a week," Charlie glowered. "These are more potent than cough syrup. However, the paranoia was very real, and Becky did catch me trying to climb out the window, so that was the end of that. In hindsight, she may have had a point."

Florin was still looking at him with an unnecessary level of judgement.

"The question, Florin, is did Lionel take these on his own merits, or did someone put them in his tea?" Charlie tried to keep them on track. "Given what I know of the man... I'm inclined to believe he was drugged."

"It would make him highly susceptible to suggestion," Amy muttered. "If someone convinced him he saw a ghost—"

"He was here!" Lionel screamed, pointing out the window. "He was right there and he told me everything!"

"All right, Lionel, I believe you," Amy began calmly. "Can you take a deep breath for me and tell me exactly what happened?"

"Pound rose from the dead, Florin!" Lionel insisted madly. "His spirit has come back to save you!"

Amy looked like she was losing her patience. Charlie didn't blame her.

"Deep breath, Lionel," Amy reminded. "Then details."

"Henry Pound Junior was right there," Lionel pointed insistently. "He was out the window, in the darkness, pale as ice, just floating… you could see the trees though him… all the little lights. He told me about Shilling… told me all the awful things he's done! Made me write it down! Made me promise I'd tell the world!"

Amy gave Charlie a bleak look as she tried to comfort Lionel. Charlie took down a wooden box from a nearby shelf, gave it a quick sniff, and then carefully pocketed it while no one was looking. Having Lionel scream at him about murder and drugs was one thing, provoking him to violence via theft was something else entirely. They had all the sense they were going to get from him and now needed to extricate themselves from the situation as carefully as possible. Charlie was backing to the door when Lionel began to yell at him again.

"I know what you're doing here, murderer!" he accused. "I know you're here to kill me!"

"No one's here to kill you, Lionel," Amy sighed. "I promise. We just wanted to know about Harry and the girl."

"Pound told me that Shilling killed her!" Lionel wept. "Now he's here to kill me!"

"I'm going to take Shilling away now, Lionel," Amy

told him carefully. "I won't let him hurt you. We're going to leave you to sober up."

Lionel didn't fight her. There were weak mutterings about her own mortal danger, about how dangerous Shilling was. Charlie watched her work like she was a disciple of Sekhmet. Her anger was only tempered by her nurture. He didn't like seeing her eyes so hard, but it was divine to behold the way she could tend to someone she clearly wanted to injure. He wondered if he had such strength in him, or if, were their positions reversed, he would just leave Lionel in a screaming heap on the floor.

Amy tucked him in and pulled the curtains, then guided Charlie from the room. The landlady was still waiting in the hallway. She had a duster in hand so that she could pretend she hadn't been eavesdropping, but her expression gave her away. Amy pulled the door shut behind them. When she sighed, her shoulders slumped like the weight of the world was rolling off them. Charlie put an arm around her and pulled her in. She slipped her arms around his waist and rested her face against his collar. The landlady looked sympathetic.

"He's been like that since yesterday," she ventured. "Screaming and ranting, going on about ghosts. Put up an awful fuss when the police came by. I'm glad they sent a doctor around."

"There might well be another later," Amy sighed, still clinging to Charlie.

"Ma'am, I don't suppose you can recall any guests Lionel's had in the last week or so?" Charlie asked.

"Doesn't really have guests," she shrugged. "Not so's I see, anyway. Tends to do his socialising elsewhere and just comes here to write and sleep."

"He seems to have been through quite the ordeal," Amy commented, rubbing her forehead wearily and turning back to the lady.

"Quite," the lady agreed. "I hate to think what he must've seen to put him like that. I s'pose if he saw that dead girl… enough to rattle anyone, I'm sure…"

"Do you know what time he was out last night?" Charlie asked.

"Oh, he was home by 9pm last night. Wasn't out late," she replied.

"He didn't go out again?" Amy checked.

"Not so's I heard," the lady shrugged. "His door's a mite squeaky, but I didn't hear it until the police showed up this morn."

"Then how did he get his story to the papers?" Charlie muttered. "Unless someone set him up for the story but he didn't actually write it…?"

"It wouldn't be hard," Amy murmured. "If the killer knew what was going to happen, if the crime was well-planned and they knew they could drug Lionel, it would be easy enough to write the story themselves, feed the nonsense to Lionel, put his name on their work and deliver it to the paper, then sit back and watch the calamity unfold. In his current state, Lionel wouldn't even know he didn't write that article, and anything he did write might be unintelligible drivel."

"We're hypothesising meticulous planning…" Charlie mused, sharing a long look with his beloved doctor.

"Given the nature of the crime, that was a guarantee," Amy frowned. She cast a glance at the landlady. "Thank you for letting us in to see him. I don't suppose we could ask you to keep an eye on any visitors he receives in the next few days?"

"I can do me best, Doctor," she agreed loyally, clearly smitten by Amy's character. Charlie didn't blame her.

"And given the ongoing nature of this official case, I hope we can trust your discretion?" Amy added.

"Of course," the landlady nodded.

Charlie decided the safest course of action was just to stay quiet and let Florin work her charm, given her present success. He settled for nodding politely and staying out of it until Amy extracted them both from the situation.

They took their leave and stepped back out into the sunshine. Charlie straightened his coat, as though to ward off the winter chill, when actually trying to hide the new weight dragging down one of his pockets. Once the door was shut and they were a safe few steps from it, he felt it necessary to voice his concern.

"You cannot trust that woman's discretion..." he warned softly.

"No," Amy agreed with a sigh, "but at least she'll feel guilty when she starts to gossip."

Charlie smiled at her with quiet admiration. Amy looked like she might never smile again, and the sight troubled him. But it was resolvable. They could fix this.

"Tanner's basically a scapegoat," Amy sighed,

rubbing her temples. "All but useless. Where to next? Bronny?"

"Hm," Charlie mused. "We do need to see her, but Lionel's not quite as useless as he may seem. First things first, I want to check the garden."

"You want to what?" Amy asked, but Charlie had already started to move away at his own declaration and she was forced to follow along as he ducked away through the trees.

They came around the side of the house where someone had made half-hearted attempts at taming the overgrown garden. It was just the minimal effort required to decorate the plants with festive cheer, but Charlie didn't wholly begrudge the attempt. It did make snooping in the garden easier. He moved slowly and carefully as he approached the area near Lionel's window. If they did anything to disturb the drugged lunatic, he would probably start screaming again, and it would be the devil's own task to calm him. More importantly, Charlie didn't want to accidentally disturb the scene of the crime.

Fallen leaves were clustered into sodden lumps at the edges of the pavers, but there wasn't enough mush to leave any decent footprints. Charlie knew that was too much to hope for anyway. No, what he was looking for was much more obscure.

Charlie was looking for evidence of Harry's ghost.

Certainly, it was safe to say that Lionel was beyond coherent thought. Charlie knew from experience that those mushrooms could make one paranoid, suggestable... see things that weren't there... but for something this specific, for something so intrinsically connected to the murder of Sarah Tuppence, there needed to have been suggestion. That meant someone needed to be here doing something to convince Lionel he'd seen a ghost, and they may not have been certain what state he would have been in.

Charlie wasn't wholly sure what he was looking for, but he knew it when he found it. Amy was giving him a strange but patient look. She had faith in his methods, even when she didn't understand why he was poking around in the dirt. But the dirt was interesting. The patterns, or — more accurately — the grooves in the mossy earth either side of the path, half hidden beneath trees and shrubs, were most illuminating. The smears of white paint on nearby leaves and the faintest fibres of pale wool were also fascinating.

"We're making one more quick stop before Bronny's," Charlie announced.

4

Amy wasn't sure what she expected, but it hadn't been this. The surprise was more pleasant than incredulous, almost whimsical. Charlie led her up the stairs to the front door of the shop and held it open for her. The small bell chimed above them as they stepped inside. She couldn't help but look around as Charlie joined her and the door jangled shut behind them. It was a dark space, plenty of nooks and crannies, and the windows were frosted artistically with grime. Everything was cluttered and there were enough stacked shelves to make her feel claustrophobic.

Of all places, they were in a magic shop. One that felt as ominous as it did mystical. Dust motes hung in the air, catching the faint light almost like microscopic flecks of crystal. Heavy velvet drapes were spaced either side of windows and between shelves, where anything or anyone could be hiding. They served as distracting bolts of shadowy, rich colour. Every which way, strange items of metal and glass and paper glinted and rustled.

Charlie moved into the store like he knew where he was going. A shuffle of footsteps moved in answer to his own. From beyond drapes over the back wall, behind the counter, came a funny little man in oriental garb. He sidled through the curtains and shuffled towards them. As soon as he caught sight of Charlie, something shifted. Amy was taken aback as the man straightened up, his stoop disappearing and his face changing. His expression moved from polite to cunning in a way that turned him into an entirely different person. A sly smile graced his lips beneath his moustache. When he spoke, she was embarrassed to admit to herself that the accent she had been expecting was not the North London one she got.

"Hello Charlie," the man smirked.

"Master Yen," Charlie bowed to him ritualistically. The action deepened Yen's smirk. He eyed them both up curiously and with a note of amusement.

"Good to see you, Shilling, and this must be Doctor Florin," Yen smiled. "Well met, Doctor." He nodded politely. Amy was too surprised by the entire experience to do more than mirror the nod. Charlie gave Yen's deduction a surprisingly dark glower, but Yen was unfazed.

"I read the papers," he said by way of explanation. "Tell me you're not here to have me make you *disappear*."

"Don't be snide," Charlie grumbled.

"You've been accused of murder most foul, Charles," Yen reminded, perching on the edge of a nearby table. "If I were you, I would have made myself very scarce until the matter was resolved."

"That's because you'd expect me to resolve it," Charlie sniffed. "Amy and I don't have the luxury of relying on someone else to solve this case."

"An unfortunate truth," Yen agreed. "So then, what does bring you here?"

"I need the names of anyone in London who has bought or rented the pieces to perform Pepper's Ghost," Charlie replied. He absentmindedly pulled a pack of cards from the shelf beside him and began to shuffle them. Amy watched his fingers work as he kept his hands busy. He was surprisingly adept. Possibly that wasn't so surprising for one who fidgeted as much as he did.

"Anyone in London?" Yen echoed incredulously. "Charlie, lad, London's a big place, I'm one magic shop, and you're talking about glass — building industry is more likely than us."

"I know," Charlie nodded, "but you have contacts. The people you know to buy from are the same ones they'd ask, presumably. Or those people might know who to ask. Besides, the buyer would need instructions on how to set it up properly. Someone will know something, and I'm starting with you."

With a small frown and twitch of an eyebrow, Yen's expression conveyed the request was fair enough.

"I can ask," he conceded. "What's this about?"

"It's about the murder," Charlie muttered bleakly. His hands were making a spectacle of riffling the cards. Amy was impressed, and she couldn't tell if he was doing it with an ulterior motive or keeping himself focused. Possibly, he was just showing off.

"Don't let him impress you, Doctor," Yen smiled at her. Amy hadn't even realised Yen was looking her way. She'd been too busy watching Charlie.

"I think it's months too late for that, Master Yen," Amy smiled with loyal affection at her sleuth.

Yen scoffed, moving behind the counter and rifling through a drawer.

"At least show the lady a trick, Shilling," he instructed.

Charlie did a basic pick-a-card trick for her. He let her choose, shuffled the deck again, and produced the card. She'd seen the trick performed enough times that it didn't surprise her he could do it.

"Is this your card?" he asked like he didn't know, all the while holding up the five of hearts.

Amy nodded in amusement. Then came the actual surprise.

"Five of Hearts, huh?" Yen commented.

Charlie shot him a dirty look, but Amy watched them with genuine curiosity. Yen was still lounging behind the counter, packing a pipe with tobacco. He glanced up briefly to smirk at them.

"Okay, hold up," Amy demanded. "The card trick is a sleight of hand ploy, I understand that much. You're on the other side of the room, how do you know what it was?"

"You are nothing if not predictable, Charles," Yen smirked. He lit his pipe and puffed gently, getting it started. "You see, Doctor, the trick is in the way he suggests to you which card to pick, placing it in a way as to make it slightly more obvious than the others. My trick, is knowing him long enough to know which card he would have picked for you. How many years,

Charlie, you still haven't changed your routine?"

"I don't practice much," Charlie shrugged. "I know this works." He riffled the cards again absentmindedly.

"You two go back a ways?" Amy inquired.

Yen grinned and blew a smoke ring at them. It grew and dissipated as it reached them.

"I taught him magic," Yen smirked.

"There's no such thing as magic," Charlie replied, sliding the cards into the box and putting them back before walking closer to Yen.

Yen rolled his eyes at Amy and she felt the exasperation in her bones. It was deeply shared. She grabbed the cards and moved to rebuke Charlie for leaving them in a mess, but as she slid them from the packet and fanned them gently, she saw they were perfectly in order. Amy blinked. That was far more impressive than the card trick. She'd seen him shuffling them! Repeatedly!

Yen was still smiling at her after she quietly put everything back. He had a knowing energy about him and she felt drawn to the mystery, but she also knew enough to know it was another in a host of tricks the magician cultivated to boost his business. This man didn't do anything garish or chic to appeal to seasonal shoppers. Celebrating Christmas would destroy the illusion of authenticity this place had. Amy was already tempted to peruse for a gift in here for Charlie. She had yet to find anything she thought suitable for him anywhere else. There would be enough shoppers who wanted the real thing – like an exotic toy shop for all ages. Yen knew his business inside and out, and he was smart enough that Charlie respected him. The respect seemed to go both ways. Charlie was investigating something else on a nearby shelf and Amy tried to catch a glimpse, but she could tell from his expression that his interest was only absentminded. Yen's eyes roved between them, and there was a fondness in the way he looked at Charlie that endeared him to Amy.

"You say that, Charlie, but you are an excellent magician," he praised nostalgically.

"I can hardly imagine you performing tricks in a cape," Amy chuckled.

"Oh God, no," Yen agreed. "He's a terrible performer. Absolutely atrocious. Excellent magician… magnificent thief." Yen shot Charlie a cunning look and Charlie ignored it completely.

"Now that, I have no trouble believing," Amy smiled.

Charlie made a small '*hmph*' sound and continued with his perusal. She watched him look, knowing that this certainly wasn't the time or place for Christmas shopping, but that it could be if she made a mental note to come back and visit Yen after the case. He might have some useful insight into her beloved sleuth. Charlie cocked his head as he looked, in that terrier way that made Amy feel like she was melting. She wanted to straighten his hair, but she wasn't wholly sure it wasn't her who'd messed it in the first place.

"You're sulking, Shilling," Yen rebuked, puffing away on his pipe. "Aside from the obvious, what's wrong?"

"Aside from the obvious?" Charlie repeated,

emphasising that the obvious was more than enough for most people.

"Something bigger is going on and you're not telling me about it," Yen stated. "You want me to keep an eye on the curtain? And ear to the ground?"

"Yes," Charlie nodded, finally abandoning his study of the trinket shelf and turning to his friend. "I do want to ask, but I don't know what to ask. I don't know what to keep an eye out for. I don't know what's going on or why, and it's bothering me."

"You're not going to find clues here," Yen shrugged. "But I can keep my attention piqued for anything suspicious."

"I'd appreciate it," Charlie gave a troubled half-frown that exaggerated the crookedness of his mouth. "A woman was brutally murdered, Master Yen; that she was killed is what troubles me most, but almost equally troubling is the disturbing notion that she was killed merely as part of a ploy to set up myself and possibly an abysmal journalist."

"What connects you and the journalist?" Yen asked, wreathed in a cloud of smoke.

"An extensive list of fabrications," Charlie sighed. "He's followed my career most diligently, yet unfaithfully. I have yet to work out if that has any direct connections to this, or if he was merely a convenient scapegoat. But someone went to a lot of trouble — with drugs, and mirrors, and glass, and someone in costume — to make that man believe he truly saw a ghost. Given the general public's disheartening gullibility and favour for superstition, even if the police aren't prepared to arrest me, the court of public opinion might lynch me."

"We won't let that happen," Amy insisted, although she knew it was her heart talking more than her head. They were already in grave trouble.

Charlie gave her a strained but grateful smile. He knew as well as she did the faults in her statement. Yen mused thoughtfully, puffing away.

"I will keep my eyes and ears open for you," he promised. "No good performer starts with their grandest feat."

"That's what worries me," Charlie grimaced. Amy shared a grim look with him. Given the nature of the crimes, it was certainly theatrical.

"And tell me, Shilling," Yen puffed on his pipe, "how fares the price of bread?"

"It's very good," Charlie smiled. "Never been better."

"Excellent," Yen smirked. "Then you shall hear from me soon. Good luck with your investigation."

Amy didn't need Charlie's advanced deductive reasoning to work that one out. She concluded, as Charlie farewelled his master and they left the shop, that Master Yen was a patron of Michael Pence's information network. It certainly explained a lot.

"Now we go to Bronny's?" Amy asked as they stepped outside.

"Can't put it off forever," Charlie muttered, like someone who might've been prepared to try if the matter wasn't so dire.

Amy slipped her hand into his and squeezed. It didn't take a magician to see he was dreading this, and she didn't blame him. He'd had to go through all this the first time, the real horror of it, and he'd promised them it was over when Harry was caught. Now they were facing the same terror again, and he couldn't tell anyone why.

There was more than one surprise waiting for Charlie at the High House, and he was grateful for all of them. The House itself was shut up for the day. No clients. But they weren't clients, and Bronny was expecting him. That was the first surprise, even if it shouldn't have been. They knocked on the locked front door, and an attractive burly man Charlie didn't recognise let them in with a gruff 'Madam's been expecting you'.

The long, curtained entrance hall had an immediate grief-stricken chill about it that contrasted starkly with the festive decorations. Despite their urgency, Charlie felt he couldn't hurry in the space, and Amy kept pace beside him. Beyond the gauze drapes and bauble-heavy garlands, Charlie glimpsed people peering at him from the stairs. Some of them he even knew. That was when Amy broke stride. She squeezed his arm once and dashed over to a mutual friend. Charlie didn't blame her. It was the right thing to do.

He had no words of comfort to give though. Comfort wasn't really in his skillset. He moved on, straight through the halls he knew so well, beelining for Bronny's office. Therein lay the next surprises. The first was most welcome and it hit him like a train.

Bronny sat behind the desk in her dim and lavish office, and she was not alone. The handsome man perched on the edge of her desk was on his feet the second Charlie opened the door.

"Where in God's name have you been?!" he demanded, crossing the room in an instant and catching Charlie in a fierce embrace. His stature and whorish, pirate-like attire meant Charlie was thrust face first into the man's open collar. He didn't particularly mind. It was nice to be held. The spiced musk of his friend's aftershave was a welcome relief from the bombardment of seasonal pine, and Julian's arms were somewhere Charlie had always felt safe. His affection was forceful, but brotherly. Even as Julian released him from the embrace, he clutched Charlie's face in both hands, still holding him close and scouring his expression with probing dark eyes. "Are you all right, Sleuth?"

Charlie nodded. "What are you doing here, Julian?"

"I came by as soon as I heard," Julian replied, slinging an arm around Charlie's shoulders and guiding him to the desk. "Which, with Skipp, you can imagine was unreasonably early. Rebecca said you weren't at home, but we figured you'd come here after you read the paper. Besides, I have resources now that I didn't have last time this happened, back when I was working here, and I wanted to volunteer them to Madam — anything you need."

"I still haven't worked out if he means his family or his husband," Bronny commented to Charlie. She was going for wry humour, but there was a tightness about her face that betrayed the simmering pain and anger. A brown paper folder sat on the desk in front of her, sheets of paper hurriedly stacked inside it. She held it out to him as he approached.

"What's this?" Charlie asked.

"Everything I've been able to gather," Bronny replied tightly.

Charlie took the folder and began to leaf through it. Another surprise, notes on the case. It had barely begun, but Bronny had compiled answers to all his initial questions, seemingly as much as she could. This close now, even in the dim light, he could see the red around her eyes that her heavy makeup sought to hide. Her mouth was so tight, as though her jaw was locked to keep it steady.

"I'm going to fix this, Bronny," Charlie promised foolishly, unable to help himself in the face of her obvious grief.

"I know, Charlie," she sighed. Bronny pressed her forehead wearily, as though in pain. Julian put a hand on her shoulder. She patted his fingers gently. "I can't do this again..." she whispered.

"The House is on lockdown again?" Charlie asked.

"Completely," Bronny answered. "No one is going out to see any clients. Ever again. Right now, I don't want anyone visiting either." She looked like she was about to say more, but stopped and just shook her head weakly.

Charlie understood. Right now, Bronny felt like the House was dying. Because it was. She wanted to close it down. A High House only existed because of the people who worked in it. This one had lost too many people. Too many women. Women who had been targeted and killed by people who were psychotically damaged. Every life had weight. Every body stacked up, and Bronny was drowning in the blood. These people were her family.

Charlie remembered that too. Everyone who lived here was someone Bronny had taken in, and she always made them welcome. He'd only been a child, but she'd been good to him. The worst he ever got was a scolding for his sleuthing. Children were not allowed near the working areas. No exceptions. But these were his people dying too, even if he hadn't ever worked for her. Even if he'd left years ago. He knew that if anything went wrong, Bronny would look after him. He wanted to return the favour, and he felt like he was failing.

He flicked through the scrawled notes in the file. Sarah had been going off to meet a 'Mister Denarius'. Charlie grimaced. Denarius was an obscenely common name — like Pence or Smith. Generic almost to the point of untraceable. But it was the same name the Jack had used. That was another deliberate indication someone was trying to copy the Jack. But *why?* Why would anyone want to copy Harry Pound's crimes? And why accuse Charlie? It didn't make any sense. Certainly, he had enemies, anyone in his line of work did, but... well... the worst of them were dead. The ones he had left were not this conniving. A bullet in a dark alley, maybe, but this... this was theatrical and personal on a level he couldn't understand.

"It says in here that Sarah had an incident with a

Master Brass?" Charlie asked.

"As in one of Lord Brass' sons," Bronny elaborated. "Derek or Duncan or something… not sure it will be relevant, but I thought it was worth mentioning. The police didn't seem interested, and I know you're always interested when they're not. It was the normal kind of altercation and I had him banned from the House afterwards. Some of those rich boys think they can treat the lower-class girls how they like."

She smiled at Charlie, and he wondered what on earth she could be smiling about, then he realised she was smiling at the dark reaction in his expression. Bronny never deliberately manipulated his war against the class system, but she did quietly approve when it served her.

"Sarah was here by circumstance, not choice?" Charlie asked.

"Everyone here is here by choice," Bronny reproved.

Charlie outstared her. Anyone who invoked his rebellion against the aristocracy had to deal with both sides of it. Bronny and her House were not above his reproval. She was good to people, but society was not built to care for its weaker members and High Houses were an out for some. If you were desirable enough, you could get a job in a High House no matter your social station, and for some that was just how they survived. That had been how Rebecca saved herself and Charlie when their father died. That was how Julian had survived after he'd run away from home. Not everyone chose it from a range of lavish options. Some chose it by circumstance. A woman called Sarah Tuppence was probably someone who chose by circumstance, even if she did enjoy where she was and what she was doing. Bronny knew that, and she didn't try and argue.

There was a knock at the door. Bronny extended an invitation, and the handsome man from the front door poked his head in.

"Uh… there's someone here, Madame Bronny," he spoke in an apologetic tone. "Someone looking for Shilling and Florin…"

Amy poured another cup of tea and brought it to the table. She tucked the blanket tighter around Lizzie's shoulders and held her while she cried. They sat together on a divan in one of the work rooms. The smell of incense worked hard to hide the other lingering scents of the space. It felt like a lifetime ago that the two of them had been close like this. Lizzie kept unconsciously touching the scar on her neck. She'd done that a lot in the early days, but Amy had watched her grow out of it. Now it was back…

"Sorry," Lizzie snuffled into her handkerchief. "You should be off helping Charlie."

"I'm sure Charlie's doing just fine," Amy assured, tightening her hand on Lizzie's shoulder a moment.

"Why does everyone blame him?" Lizzie cried. "Why's everyone saying it's his fault? Charlie'd never!"

"No, he wouldn't," Amy sighed, taking Lizzie in her arms and swaying gently. "But it was a deliberate attack against him. Someone is trying to set him up."

"Someone killed Sarah just to get at Charlie?!" Lizzie exclaimed, pained outrage straining her voice.

"It looks horribly like it," Amy murmured, loath that she had to tell Lizzie that another one of her friends was dead because of her and Charlie. It hadn't been Charlie's fault the first time. It wasn't his fault this time. There was a niggling part of Amy's soul that, while able to make that important distinction for him, would never stop blaming herself a little bit for the women Harry had killed.

"The police are saying it's a copycat…" Lizzie muttered, wiping her eyes. "Someone else trying to be the Jack…" Her lip trembled. "Is that what life is now? We just close down all the High Houses because there's always going to be some sick monster who wants to stalk and kill women?"

"I don't know what it's going to look like," Amy sighed. "But I don't think it will get that far. No one wants the High Houses to shut. We just have to work a little harder to keep our ladies safe for now, and then things can go back to normal…" she felt like a liar even as the word escaped her lips.

"That's what everyone said after the Jack," Lizzie muttered. "Now we got this."

"You're right," Amy sighed. "Of course you're right. I can't promise you normal, I can't promise you safety, or that the world will miraculously become a good place where we don't have to be afraid of bad people, but I can promise you this: Charlie and I caught the first Jack, we'll catch this one too."

Lizzie nuzzled into her gratefully and kissed her cheek. Amy just sighed again and held her close, stroking her hair and hoping that she was able to ease, even mildly, the trauma of a friend who had lost another House sister to a twisted killer.

They were still sitting that way, tea untouched, when there was a knock at the door, calling Doctor Florin to come and meet some unexpected visitors at the door.

Charlie met Amy in the corridor as they both responded curiously to their respective summons. Bronny and Julian came with him, and they paused temporarily while Julian gave Amy a customary bear hug. Charlie could see the strain of Lizzie's grief on Amy's face. Her ability to care for others was awe inspiring, but looking at the toll of it sometimes made him grateful he didn't know how to do it himself. He was still carrying the folder Bronny had given him. If this was the police, he was prepared to share information. Potentially.

However, what met them in the entrance hall was utterly unexpected. Perhaps it shouldn't have been, but Charlie was prepared to admit he was surprised. Amy clearly even more so.

"Oh my God!" she exclaimed, as soon as she saw the two women sitting on the divan behind one of the many Christmas trees. "What are you doing here?! You're supposed to be getting ready for the wedding!"

"So are you," Jane pointed out, sitting demurely

with her cheeky bride giving Amy an imperious look beside her.

"I'm sorry..." Amy apologised as they reached Jane and Laura. "Truly, I am so sorry..."

"I'm sorry," Charlie cut over her, standing protectively at her side and trying to take some of the blame from her friends. "I'm sorry I dragged her away—" he apologised.

"Oh?" Laura looked Amy up and down. Her expression was challenging, almost smug, but that didn't seem right and Charlie wasn't sure if he just couldn't read it. He had no quarrel with Amy's friends, and they were right to be angry, but... they didn't seem angry, and Charlie didn't understand... and all he could figure out right now was that the way Laura eyeballed Amy made him uncomfortable.

"Dragging her? You two into bondage now?" Laura asked him boldly. "I don't see a leash, Shilling, and if there was one, I honestly thought you'd be wearing it."

"Wha—?! How is that—?!" Charlie stammered, trying to work out what possible mental leap had been made there that he could not follow. The pedantry of her response was logical and he probably would have found it amusing... had it been about someone else. "I'm... sorry...?"

Amy, of course, was used to her friends. She not only wasn't flummoxed by them, but she was losing patience too. Perhaps unfairly, Charlie thought, although he wasn't going to tell her how to feel, especially after the morning they'd had. He watched her glorious green eyes settle with bitter irritation.

"Charlie's apologising because he feels responsible for the situation, not for my behaviour," she defended brusquely. "I'm sorry I abandoned you when you needed me. It was an action unworthy of your friendship and you deserve better, but I wouldn't change the decision. A woman is dead and I am certain more lives are in danger. Charlie and I are doing what we can, but it is not so easy when the court of public opinion is hunting him like a fox. Please be gentle with him."

"She's teasing you, not attacking you, Amelia," Jane mediated. "Take a breath, darling."

"We're here to collect you, not reprimand you," Laura agreed. "But it's my wedding day, I'm allowed to tease my friends."

"I… I can't—" Amy started to protest.

"You can," Charlie interrupted. He tucked the folder under his arm and took her hand in both of his, meeting her gaze gently. "What will you regret more, Florin? Not helping with every second of this case, or missing your best friends' wedding? I will tell you everything I find—"

"What makes you think you're not coming too, Mister Shilling?" Laura demanded.

Charlie blushed. "Well, I— uh, I— after… after the paper this morning… you surely can't want…"

"Okay, so here's the thing," Laura interrupted with an allusion of patience that wasn't being displayed, "they don't get to win. My bride and I were having a little chat while we waited and— heh, my *bride*," Laura repeated, getting distracted by the word and going all soft and doe-eyed.

"What my darling is trying to say," Jane took over with an affectionate smile, "is that this isn't just about you two. We knew Sarah."

Everyone paused. Jane and Laura shared a look. There was a lot in it. Too much to read. Certainly too much for Charlie to read, although he tried. There was love and devotion and sadness and determination. The two brides squeezed each other's hands reassuringly.

"Sarah used to work in the Tuppence Teahouse down in Westminster, before she came here," Laura told them. "We used to see quite a bit of her there and we knew her quite well."

"We're sorry for your loss," Bronny told them softly.

"We're sorry for everyone's loss!" Laura exclaimed. "What happened to Sarah is the worst kind of nightmare, but I guarantee you the last thing Sarah would want is to know that her friends are locked up mourning her or skipping out on their promises to avenge her, especially while her killer is out there."

"You can't cancel the wedding," Amy blurted.

"We're not cancelling anything," Jane agreed. "We're expanding. We can certainly cater for it, and it's the right thing to do — for Sarah."

"You're going to catch the bastard who did this, Amy," Laura insisted. "I know you are, sweetheart. But you're not going to do it tonight, and we're not going to let the people who did this win. We're not going to let them make your Charlie public enemy number one. We're not going to let them scare the High Houses into lockdown. If your ladies can't go anywhere alone for fear of what might happen, then you all come as a group! Come spend our wedding with us. Come celebrate tonight, and then next week we can go to Sarah's memorial together. Let's make her memory bigger than the Jack's. Let's make sure that whoever's trying to hurt us doesn't get to, that Sarah gets honoured instead of used as a tool to make people scared."

Charlie and Amy shared a look. Amy looked like she wanted to cry and that did terrible things to Charlie's insides. He could see why she was moved by her friend's speech. It was certainly rousing, though he wasn't sure it was practical. He was honoured that they wanted to help him, even on behalf of Sarah and Amy, and a small, niggling echo of Master Yen's voice egged him on to acceptance. It was Amy who spoke though.

"You two..." she shook her head, misty-eyed, and stepped forward to clasp their hands. The three of them stood in a triangle of mutual adoration. "You are so kind... but I don't want to risk dragging the focus of your wedding off of you. It's supposed to be your day!"

"It is our day," Laura insisted. "That's why we should get what we want."

"And we don't mind bringing along some distractions and sacrificing some focus," Jane smiled, "especially if it keeps our mothers from making it all about them."

Another look was shared, this time between the three of them. Charlie was only a witness, but it looked bad. He heard Bronny give the slightest sigh of a chuckle behind her hand.

"Darling, are you avoiding your mother?" Amy asked.

"She's staging a coup," Laura defended.

"And we'd never want to force anyone to do something they didn't want to," Jane insisted, "but can you imagine Lady Mark's face if we convince everyone to join us? My mother would also have a fit." She looked terribly pleased about that.

"Amy," Laura let go of her bride to hold both of Florin's hands. "We know what you're doing is important. We know you wouldn't have run out on us this morning if it wasn't. You know us well enough to know that if another woman died because you were at our wedding instead of hunting the killer, we could never forgive ourselves. We can't protect everyone in the city, but we can do our part to protect the people in immediate danger and give them somewhere safe to go. That includes you and Shilling too."

Amy turned to look at him. Charlie felt like she expected him to have an answer, which was ridiculous as it was *her* friends' wedding... the funny thing was, he did have one. He gave her a slow nod. She seemed as surprised by it as he was.

"You need to be there, Florin," he insisted. "Your friends make a strong case with admirable intention, and our excuses have run dry. I can put out a few more feelers, but most of our leads require patience for now anyway. If we are to pass our time waiting for information, there's no good reason not to pass that time at the wedding."

Everyone seemed surprised by his answer. He was a

little surprised by his answer, but it was the only thing that made sense.

"Charlie… can I have a word with you?" Amy asked.

He nodded and followed her back towards the corridor. She pulled him aside behind one of the many festive trees lining the hall, this one decorated with red and white. He stifled a sneeze at the overwhelming scent of pine. Behind them, Bronny was agreeing to take the brides' proposal to the House, and Julian was wrangling an invite for himself and Michael. It didn't take much wrangling.

"Florin," Charlie spoke softly as soon as they had some semblance of privacy, "if you're looking for an out, I'm reluctant to help you find one—"

"I'm not looking for an out, Charlie," she whispered, standing exhilaratingly close in that way she did that made his head spin. It wasn't just allergies. "You're right. This case is driving me a bit mad, but if I missed their wedding, I would regret it for the rest of my life. I have to go with them, but I'm reluctant to drag you along if I know you have a case to obsess over. Do you really want to go?"

"I do," he nodded. She still looked uncertain, so he tried to find the words to explain the storm of emotions and calculations he was trying to process. "I have a number of reasons to believe this is the right thing to do. The first and most obvious is that it is what your friends appear to want, and my understanding of matrimonial events are that the betrothed are to be catered to."

Amy gave him a smile. It was one of those smiles. The kind that she'd been giving him since they met.

That mysterious smile she gave him whenever he cocked his head or stated the obvious. He really felt he ought to know what it meant by now. Maybe it just meant that she liked him. No, it couldn't be that simple.

"Obviously, there are other reasons as well, reasons that could genuinely help with the case, but… well… I… I suppose… the most evident and prominent reason is that it's important to you," he did his best to explain. "It's important to you, so that makes it important to me."

"Charlie… that's dangerously romantic," she warned him teasingly.

"It's not dangerous on purpose," he promised.

All ability to reason was lost as she placed her hand on his cheek and kissed him. This was probably the most prominent motivation he had for agreeing to attend the wedding, but he was sure there were others. The trick was going to be remembering them once he was there. Especially if there was going to be more kissing.

5

The horrors of the morning felt like a strange nightmare Amy had finally woken from. She had left Charlie with Julian, who was under strict instructions to look after him and get him to the wedding. She had gone with her friends and now she was helping to put the finishing touches on Jane's dress and hair. Jane's sisters were in a tizz, because their mother was in a tizz, because Jane and Laura had just announced that they were expecting another sixty guests. The brides were unconcerned, unbothered, and confident that there was enough of everything to cover it. They seemed to be enjoying the drama of their families coming to terms with the development.

Amy smiled as she pinned the last of Jane's curls in place and set them with deep green leaves, like a dryad queen. Both brides had gone for green detailing on their dresses and in their hair, with predominantly green bouquets. The bridesmaids were in cream and a pale olive that was nearly pistachio. Green suited Amy just fine, and it was a good colour for her friends too. It was a colour of new beginnings.

"What are you thinking about?" Jane smiled. She placed a hand over the one Amy had left on her shoulder, and turned from the looking glass to face her.

"I was thinking about how beautiful you look," Amy smiled back, planting a careful kiss on Jane's cheek. "And how lucky Laura is."

Jane smiled warmly at her, but there was something penetrating behind the look.

"Tell me what you're really thinking," she requested.

"That is what I'm really thinking!" Amy laughed. "Truly, I have left the morning behind me, and I am going to make the most of that for however long I can. Misery loves company, I'm sure, but it can do without mine for now." Jane's look was unrelenting and Amy cocked an eyebrow. "If I must speak of something else to convince you, I don't suppose you have any ideas for what one might gift an anti-capitalist with very few desires for Christmas?"

Jane shrugged pensively. "A goat?" she suggested.

"I do not wish to alienate his sisters," Amy laughed, although she was privately certain Charlie would love a pet goat.

"Fair enough," Jane chuckled. "Turn and let me fix the bow at the back of your dress. I can see it going lopsided from here."

"I'm the one supposed to be fixing you up," Amy reminded as she turned.

"Yes, but I look perfect now," Jane replied smugly.

"You're welcome," Amy retorted, matching Jane's tone but unable to keep the amused giggle from her voice. It felt strange to have Jane fussing over her now. It felt strange to have anyone fussing over what she wore these days. Most of her days were spent with Charlie, and she'd never met anyone who cared less what people wore. It was a refreshing change.

The thought was like a bucket of ice water over her head.

"There is it," Jane breathed.

"Bow's fixed?" Amy checked, trying to force joviality through the strain.

"Nearly," Jane replied, pulling tightly at the sash around Amy's corset. "I was talking about the rising darkness I keep catching behind your eyes."

Amy turned her head to look over her shoulder. Jane wasn't even looking in her eyes. How could she possibly know what was going on? Maybe it was just her intuition. Maybe they'd just known each other so many years that the feelings unravelled themselves.

"You want to tell me what you're really thinking…?" Jane asked.

"No…" Amy whispered.

Jane wrapped her arms around Amy and hugged her from behind, holding her close and kissing her cheek.

"Stop being scared of ruining my day," Jane whispered with a smile. "You don't have that kind of power."

A soft choke of laughter escaped Amy's throat, but it sounded more like a blubber.

"Do you think it would have been like this…?" she whispered, half convinced Jane wouldn't let her go until she admitted something. "If I'd married Harry… do you think it would have been a wedding like this? That we'd be just like this, but our roles reversed? If we'd never found out the truth… do you think I could have done it? God… what would it have been like if I'd gone through with it? If I'd married him and never known…"

Jane held her tightly, her arms squeezing reassuringly.

"The only answer I can give feels like the most important one," she sighed, "and that is the comforting thought that we will never have to know."

Amy sighed deeply and relaxed in Jane's embrace. She was right, of course.

"You don't miss him, do you?" Amy asked. "You don't miss how it used to be?"

"I don't miss Harry," Jane sniffed. "I found him uncomfortably possessive of you. I think… I think I worry about you more now, we both do, but it's a different kind of worry."

"Charlie would never hurt me," Amy defended immediately.

"If there was even a sliver of doubt, he wouldn't be invited to the wedding," Jane smiled, releasing Amy and turning her to face her. "But you have nearly gotten yourself killed chasing after him before, and Harry's ghost is still chasing you. That's enough to make anyone worry."

"There's no such thing as ghosts," Amy promised, squeezing Jane's shoulders.

"Regardless of the absolute fiction that passes for tabloids these days," Jane countered, "you still don't have closure with your past, darling. You're standing with me now, thinking about him, letting him take up space in your mind. That's plenty enough to pass for a ghost. Amy... do you miss Harry?"

Amy stared at her shoes. They were beautiful cream slippers with cosy fur trim that she wasn't sure would survive the garden wedding this evening. Perhaps she should have asked for something a bit more robust. Or perhaps she would just take it gently in her Maid of Honour attire. The dress did not exactly lend itself to athletics, it was built to be beautiful.

Unlike her silence. Her absolutely damning silence.

"Sometimes..." she whispered, consumed with shame.

"That's okay," Jane told her, clutching her arms reassuringly. "I know you don't hear that much, but it is okay, Amy. I think you have spent a lifetime forbidden from acknowledging the truth, because you and Harry always catered to what was expected of you. He was your family, darling. He and his father are the only family you ever knew, and you were never allowed to call him your brother because society had plans for the two of you, but he was. He was your brother, Amy, which is probably why you didn't want to marry him, but... but you loved him even if you were never in love with him. Who he was didn't just dry up and blow away overnight, even if in the harsh light of truth it feels like it did. I know the world needs him to be a one-dimensional villain for them to hate now, that people need him to be the devil, but he wasn't that. Amelia, sweetheart, you are allowed to miss him, and you are allowed to acknowledge what he was to you, and you are allowed to mention him without fear of judgement — even if only to Laura and myself."

Amy felt like she should cry. She felt like she should throw herself in Jane's lap and weep. But her eyes were dry. Her heart was clear. She took a deep breath like all the pressure in the world was coming off her chest. She threw her arms around Jane and squeezed her with all the love and gratitude that was exploding out of her.

"I can't believe how lucky I am to have friends like you two," she exclaimed softly. "I can't believe how blessed I am, that God in all her endless grace, saw fit to make my best friends the wisest and most wonderful women in England — and I can't believe I nearly missed your wedding because I was still feeling guilty about Harry. I am so sorry!"

"You're already forgiven," Jane kissed her cheek again, both careful not to smear their makeup. "And you're here now. That's all that matters."

"Then let's go see you safely married," Amy grinned, squeezing Jane's hands in both of hers. Jane's smile matched her own, possibly even outshone it. Her brown curls set with a floral crown made her look like an angel. She was an angel. Amy was certain of it. If ghosts could manifest as her guilt for Harry, angels could manifest as best friends.

"Charlie, you are not a terrier! Stop growling!" Rebecca ordered. She had him clasped around the middle and was holding him tightly to keep him from leaping at

Julian. Julian was standing in the corner of Charlie's bedroom, safely positioned behind towering piles of hoarded junk, holding Charlie's pale, ratty coat. He had dressed up his own usual black with royal blues and emerald greens that made him look like the world's most promiscuous peacock. It was unclear whether the alarm creasing the corners of his eyes was from the notion Charlie might bite or having to hold the ragged, stained garment.

"Give!" Charlie insisted, straining against his sister's clutches.

"No, Charlie, we talked about this," Rebecca insisted. "You can't have the coat. Not tonight."

"You let me wear it to the Sterling wedding!" Charlie protested.

"Yes," Rebecca relented, still holding him back. "But it wasn't quite so bad back then. It's had a lot more blood stains since then, it's been stomped and kicked and scraped— Charlie! It's had a burning building fall on it, and it's crawled through the sewers! Charlie! Stop!"

"Don't make her set Jasper on you, Sleuth," Julian warned.

"I wouldn't do that," Becky grunted, still trying to subdue her wriggling worm of a little brother.

The admission stilled something in him. He stopped struggling. He let her sit him on edge of his bed and straighten his waistcoat. Rebecca never made him interact with Jasper anymore if she could help it. The notion brought a very cold and primal fear to her eyes. She tried to hide it, but Charlie could see it, and it made him feel guilty. He couldn't tell her that. It would only make things worse. He had spent years keeping the truth from her because he knew it would do this. Sometimes, it felt like she was more traumatised than he was. He understood, he was confident he understood, but it was unhelpful.

"Here you go, Charlie," Rebecca said softly, draping a coat around his shoulders. "This one should be acceptable. Remember, it's only for tonight."

Charlie nodded. Only for tonight. If it wasn't an event he was already anxious about, the coat would probably have been an easier barrier to overcome. The problem was the aggravation to his already heightened emotions. Rebecca knew his customary tics well. The new coat was a more tailored fit. He could live with that. It was olive green. Nothing garish. Not like Julian. The fabric was soft, not too scratchy. It was... acceptable. He reached out slowly and stimmed a button.

No.

The buttons were all wrong. Wrong shape. Wrong texture. Not comforting at all. Something must have shown in his face. Rebecca took his fingers from the coat and set them against his ring. Better. He stimmed the ring, circling the smooth edge of the signet circle.

"Just for tonight, Charlie," Rebecca repeated patiently.

He nodded.

Across the room, Julian set the coat down carefully, now that no one was worried Charlie might bite someone to get it. Charlie could feel his friend watching him, but couldn't look up to meet his eye. He dropped his gaze to his ring and watched his finger circle and circle and circle like a bird that never quite came in to land. Surely, some point soon, he would be calm enough to stop.

"Remember," Rebecca whispered, kissing his forehead gently, "you're doing this for Amy. On a scale of things you've done for her… this ranks fairly low."

Charlie almost smiled. His finger came to a slow and gradual stop, slipping from the metal to rest on Rebecca's hand. He looked up, affectionately planting a soft kiss on his sister's cheek, and then stood with quiet resolve. He slipped his arms into the sleeves of his jacket. His eyes turned slowly to Julian who was regarding him carefully.

Downstairs, there was a knock at the door. Charlie and Julian shared a look.

"That'll be Skipp," Charlie sighed.

"Right on time," Julian smiled. "I should have known it would take the same length of time to get you two ready to attend a wedding."

"I'll go get the carriage prepared," Rebecca offered.

She was out the door before she could glimpse Charlie's frown, which was probably a blessing. It bothered him when people used terminology that implied they were completing work that they were actually forcing others to do for them. But that was a fight he had with Rebecca every other day, and today they could do without it.

Charlie checked his pockets, patting himself down slowly. Handkerchief, keys, notebook, purse… he quickly added lockpicks, string, wire, and a lighter. You could never be too careful, even at a wedding. He led Julian from his room and shut the door with a click behind them. They reached the landing just as Jasper reached the front door. As they came down the stairs, Charlie smiled at the vision of Michael in the doorway, respectably clad in blue. He looked as uncomfortable in his finery as Charlie felt in his own. Julian was going to have his hands full managing the common folk tonight. He didn't look concerned. He practically swept down the stairs to collide with his husband. Michael's hand was already drifting unconsciously to his scarred cheek, and Julian made sure his lips got their first, catching Michael gently in the doorway.

That left Charlie to stand with Jasper in the entrance, looking on.

"Jasper," he gave the man a polite nod.

"Master Shilling," Jasper replied with reverence and a bow that, like usual, never met Charlie's eyes anymore. Charlie didn't have the energy for that dance today; he had to save his strength in case someone required that he actually dance later. Jasper never gave him any trouble these days. Charlie didn't miss the pranks, but he wasn't sure he was fond of the reverence either. He would concede that he missed the attitude. Jasper's attitude, while infuriating, was at least invigorating, and his wit sharp — when he was prepared to use it. The only people in the house who stood up to Charlie now were his sisters. One of whom he'd been bickering with since he was born, and the other who didn't so much stand up to him as step on him. Charlie's indignation at class oppression always seemed to squelch unpleasantly beneath his sister-in-law's boot.

"Apologies, I didn't mean to keep you waiting," Michael said.

"You didn't, Skipp," Charlie assured him. "Believe me, I was having my own private breakdown upstairs. At least you were working."

"Only a few last-minute things to attend to," Mike replied. Charlie could feel his friend's eyes scouring him for any sign of the aforementioned weakness, or what might've caused it. "All sorted now. Of course, I don't like walking out on the job for the evening any more than you do."

"Then let's not think of it as walking out," Charlie replied, steeling himself as he led his friends around to the stables where Rebecca was overseeing the preparation of the carriage. He had personally been inclined to find other arrangements, but Rebecca was insistent that they do things properly tonight. Charlie was begrudging in his agreement and attempting to pretend it wasn't as wholehearted as it felt. He did not want to do what he was about to do, but given that he was doing it, they may as well do it right.

Julian kept a hand on Michael the entire way. Charlie couldn't quite tell if it was because he was worried Mike might try and bolt from an evening of small-talk, or if, far more likely, he just struggled to keep his hands to himself when he was with his husband. At least it helped to distract from the way Michael was looking at Charlie. He could feel his friend's eyes on his back like a prickling stem of nettles.

They didn't speak again until they were all settled in the carriage and it was rumbling across the cobbles down the street. Charlie sat backward in the enclosed space, facing his friends who were tangled together in a manner that satisfied Julian's need for affection. Julian was pressed against Mike's side, clinging to him as he hungrily kissed Michael's jawline.

"We're not alone in here," Mike reminded him.

"Charlie doesn't mind," Julian smirked, refusing to take his lips from Mike's skin.

Charlie didn't mind… depending how far Julian wanted to take it. There had been a time, it felt not so long ago, when he had been prepared to lock the two of them in a cupboard until they kissed. Fortunately, it hadn't come to that, and it was nice to be assured that they were still safely infatuated with each other. Still, he wasn't the kind of person who was ever going to be interested in watching his friends have sex. At least Skipp wasn't the kind to appreciate an audience. Julian was their only wild card, and he wasn't the type to push their boundaries so intensely — however enthusiastic it was starting to look. If nothing else, it gave Charlie something to practice drowning out. He was going to have the devil's own trouble filtering the chaos tonight. If he couldn't even ignore these two, he wasn't going to cope with a crowd.

"You've got that look on your face, Sleuth," Mike warned softly.

"It's a rather—" Julian began cheekily.

"Don't finish that sentence, Swift," Skipp ordered.

His blue eyes were cold, almost hard. They were iced with deep concern. He was still staring at Charlie. "I know that look, Sleuth. If I didn't know better, I'd say that's the look of someone preparing to kill."

"Worse," Charlie grimaced. "Preparing to talk to people."

Both his friends grinned at him. Julian even tore his attention from his husband to laugh in Charlie's direction.

"You're excellent at talking to people, Sleuth," he smirked.

"No," Charlie shook his head. "I'm excellent at observing and listening to people while they talk at me. I'm not good at being the one doing the talking."

"You are when it's about class warfare," Mike smiled.

"Or in defence of Florin," Julian added.

"Or for a job," Skipp finished. He was still eyeing Charlie with acute awareness. "You're still working."

Charlie met his look, but didn't hold it. He dropped his gaze to straighten his cuff.

"*Ooohohoh,*" Julian untangled himself from Mike to regard Charlie properly. "We're not going to this wedding for the sake of the good doctor?"

"Two things can be true," Charlie replied, ignoring the faint worm of guilt that curled in the pit of his stomach.

"Don't hide this from us, Sleuth," Skipp ordered. "This wedding will be full of rich aristocrats — Amy's people. There was an awful lot of crossover with Amy's people and Harry's people. You think this killer is tied to Pound Junior?"

"Everything about this case is tied to him," Charlie replied. "You can't copy a killer's work without making the new murder about them. Whoever killed Sarah Tuppence wanted to send a message, presumably to me, given Lionel's article and the fact that I caught Harry."

"Are we sure about Harry though?" Julian asked. "I mean, given that the entire affair seems to be an extensive effort to besmirch your name, could it just be that the Jack of Hearts is your most infamous case?"

"Perhaps," Michael conceded, still staring at Charlie. "That's not impossible, but you have reason to think otherwise, don't you, Sleuth?"

Charlie thought for a moment, rubbing his mouth as he tried to compile his thoughts.

"All rivers flow to the ocean. All roads lead to Rome. What have you heard?" he asked.

"I'm still trying to gain traction on the missing weapon that's disappeared from evidence," the Skipper admitted. "Not knowing when it vanished is making things harder, but I have a couple of people on the inside. We'll have to get back to you on that, but it certainly implicates a strong tie to the original Jack. With regard to your specific besmirching, I know Lionel was being fed, but I don't know who was doing the feeding. He never went anywhere near the scene of the crime, never spoke to police. Aside from the story in the papers, he hasn't had a single connection to the case or anyone looking into it, which could be why the police aren't taking him seriously — except for an official warning against publishing slander and false information in an attempt to instigate a panic. They've told him one more unsubstantiated article and they'll book him." Mike gave Charlie a sly look. "Some perks to sharing the bed of the daughter of the Lord Chief Justice."

Charlie did not smile.

"I've got a couple of people keeping an eye on that as well, just in case," Skipp continued. "Thing is, we all know Lionel's a worm. He has spent years stirring up dirt and filth and trying to make more of it than it is. This… this is new even for him, and he's not digging himself. I do wonder if something happened to him… possibly blackmail. It smells like blackmail, but I can't find any trace of it."

Charlie dug through his pockets for his notebook and brought it out, flipping to a small sketch he'd traced earlier when he'd gotten home. He held it out for them.

"That's the logo of a gentlemen's club…" Skipp mused, although he didn't sound certain.

"Smoke & Arrow, over in Westminster, near Parliament," Julian offered. The other two shot him a look and he shrugged. "There's some overlap between the members there and the House's clients."

"Anyone you serviced?" Charlie asked.

Julian almost seemed to close up. The hand he had resting on Michael's leg tightened in what was a barely perceptible twitch, and his smile became guarded.

"Not kissing and telling, Sleuth. Even for you," he answered.

That was a 'yes', Charlie deduced. Not an interesting

one, though. Julian was always shy about his more amorous work in front of Michael.

"If you're looking for overlap though," Julian added, "Harry Pound was a member. In fact, quite a few of his LOAM friends still are."

"Not a particularly welcoming space for you then? Some of your more closeted clients?" Charlie checked.

Julian glowered. He looked more put out that Charlie was, as they all called it, 'doing a Charlie' on him and not respecting his previous attempt to hold back disclosures. Michael did an admirable job of covering his laugh with a cough.

"Aye, it caters to the more boring side of London's aristocracy," Swift grumbled. "And the more bigoted. It's a respectable enough place, but the members are the type to box women into whores, wives, and the Queen. They can't get more imaginative than that."

"Something to look into without Doctor Florin, then," Mike suggested. "Although, she does still have quite the way with Harry's LOAM friends. A fair few of them still treat her like she was his wife."

Charlie didn't know what showed on his face. He didn't know how he felt about that statement, other than that he knew it to be true. Michael and Julian were watching him though. He wasn't sure if their curiosity was satisfied with his reaction, and he didn't care.

"There was a box in Lionel's apartment with this symbol on it," he told them. "It was full of laced tea. Lionel had been drugged quite intensely when we saw him. It doesn't sound like it was a good trip, but it did make him hugely susceptible to the concept of me as a serial killer."

"Lionel's not a member," Julian replied instantly. "There's no way those men would let someone like him in."

"He is a thief though," Skipp mused.

"He's also a chump," Charlie sighed. "Lionel likes to gossip about and ruin people he considers more successful than himself. He likes to brown nose, and he likes to degrade those of lower social standing in an attempt to emulate the worst of the aristocracy and associate with them."

"You think he's being set up?" Mike raised an eyebrow. "Someone's using him?"

"Sarah was killed like she was nothing," Charlie murmured. "Just a pawn in someone's game. A piece to sacrifice to further an agenda. I don't know what that agenda is yet. I don't know how it involves me. However, I do know that those who play like they have pawns never just have one. Lionel is a piece on the board, and he's nobody's king. He's not even a rook."

"Does this have anything to do with your visit to Yen today?" Mike inquired. He met Charlie's look with a condescending smirk that had a noticeable effect on Julian. "Of course I know about it, Sleuth."

"Lionel's being used," Charlie sighed. "Whoever's doing it has ties to Bronny's House and to the Smoke & Arrow club, and probably ties to Harry Pound."

"Harry Pound rubbed a lot of shoulders," Julian commented. "He was a Lord's son and a popular one besides."

"I haven't narrowed it down yet, but tonight might

be a good opportunity," Charlie admitted.

"What's the plan?" Michael asked.

Charlie pursed his lips in momentary discomfort before answering.

"We lie," he replied. "People are going to want to know what I'm doing at this wedding. When they ask, we explain that the police investigation into Sarah's death has uncovered proof that Lionel was blackmailed into writing that story and that I have no ties to the case."

"That's barely a lie, Sleuth," Julian commented. "Why are you so stressed?"

"The key to a good lie, my love, is burying it in truth," Michael explained carefully, his fingers drifting to his scars. Julian caught his hand and pulled it away, kissing his cheek. Michael let him, watching Charlie carefully and calculating the situation. "You're going to throw the stick and see which dogs chase it. Excellent work, Charles. It's a good plan, but you do risk causing a commotion at the wedding — the wedding of the two closest, dearest, most treasured friends of the woman you love."

"Aye, right," Julian grimaced. "Yeah, I'd be shitting myself too."

"Thanks, Swift," Charlie muttered sarcastically. "Amazing vote of confidence."

"We're here for you, Charlie," Michael promised with a smile. "We're just aware caution is required, and no one wants to curse you by making optimistic declarations."

"Like you've ever been superstitious in your life,

Skipp," Charlie scoffed.

Michael gave him a smug, non-committal shrug that pulled noticeably at Julian's attention.

"The important thing," Mike began patiently, like he was talking to them both from his Skipper's chair back in his office, "is that we move quietly. Carefully. We do this, but we all do it on our absolute best behaviour." He shot his husband a very direct look. "Best behaviour, Jules. Think you can manage that?" The challenge should never have been issued and they all knew it. Michael regretted it almost instantly. "Julian—!" His protests were soon muffled as his husband pounced on him and tried to force his tongue down Mike's throat.

Charlie permitted himself a small chuckle as he looked away. Skipp had decreed no one say it aloud, but he couldn't help but wonder as he tried to tune out his friends wrestling across the carriage from him, what could possibly go wrong?

6

Amy would have been lying if she said she expected the wedding to go off without a hitch. Ignoring the drama of Jane and Laura's families, and weddings in general, she was used to having things turn to disaster in front of her now.

But it didn't. It went perfectly, as though all her silent prayers on the way to the ceremony had been answered. She knew the brides had been hoping for snow, hence a Christmastime wedding. Although, her experience of snow was never as romantic as it seemed, and this was preferable. She also had a sneaking suspicion that they had only wanted to bring their families together once a year at most, but didn't want to tell them that. So the greatest disaster of the wedding seemed to be that the weather had stayed fine. The worst she personally encountered was a congregation of ladies discussing the Florence Pound book, and that had been easy enough to walk away from. She was waiting for the other shoe to drop. Obviously, if anything was going to turn to disaster, it was going to do so at the reception.

The reception was the part of the night she was most looking forward to, because it was the only part of the event she would get to share with Charlie. She was glad he had his friends to keep him company. If she'd dragged him to a wedding and abandoned him with socialites, the guilt would have been overwhelming. Also, as much as she loved him, she didn't trust him not to attempt to overthrow the aristocracy and offend everyone in attendance if left to his own devices.

The reception was being held at Jane's family estate, so it was some travel from the church, but no one seemed to mind. Amy and the brides made a point of testing some of the champagne on the way there, and the journey was rather pleasant. The Franc Estate was lavish at the best of times, and today the gardens had been decorated specially.

Candles, lanterns, and small fires lit the garden magically as everyone gathered about in their finest furs. A small band was set up near the main fountain, and the sound of violins drifted across the paved dance floor and extensive seating area. If anyone had been shocked by the arrival of so many extra guests, there was no sign of it here. Someone had even put floral arrangements around the entrance of the hedge maze as an invitation to those who wanted to spend their evening lost in the bushes.

Amy was waiting to greet guests as they arrived, and she saw Julian eye the maze as the men approached. The sight of them coming down the path was hilarious to anyone who knew them. Julian strolled in the middle like an eccentric and flamboyant Lord, while Michael and Charlie were practically dragged in his wake either side of him like two small, blonde, and incredibly anxious attendants.

"Amy!" Julian crowed delightedly at the sight of her, coming in for a bear hug.

"Hello Julian," she smiled, swallowed up in his embrace. Hugging Julian always made her feel the tiniest flicker of jealousy for Michael, but it wasn't a real sensation. Just an appreciation for the man's warm arms and handsome smile. "I take it there was wine involved in your journey too?"

"The tiniest bit," he replied, letting her go and holding his thumb and forefinger apart with only the merest smidgen of a gap. A blatant lie.

Amy laughed at him and gave Michael a polite nod of greeting, which Skipp returned graciously. She had never received anything but quiet respect from Charlie's best friend, but she could tell she made him nervous. Not as nervous as large crowds made him, but the spymaster was the definition of guarded, and he preferred the company of the five people in the world he actually trusted.

Then Charlie was there. He came in close, as though gravitating towards her, but his posture was hesitant. There was no sign or previous experience to explain to him what was appropriate in this situation. She decided to solve that dilemma for him, drawing him in gently as she placed a hand on his arm. He sank towards her as though falling into a safety net, his expression grateful for the rescue.

Charlie wore his appreciation large in his eyes, grey like misty rain. Before she even realised she was doing it, Amy pulled him into a kiss. Her hands cupped his face and she breathed deeply as she pressed her lips to his. He smelled good. He'd washed and shaved before the wedding. A luxury they had not been afforded at the beginning of their day. Her fingers traced his jaw, across the faintest texture of fine stubble as she tried to resist messing his hair. Someone had gone to the effort of fixing it, after all. The only someone who could get away with it, and Florin was grateful. Rebecca would have dressed him. No one else could make Charlie conform.

She could feel him start to tense in her hands and didn't know if she was holding him for too long. He was always a touch shy with an audience, and his friends were probably smirking at them. He tasted sober. There was none of the wine on his breath that she had smelled on Julian. Of course. And she'd been drinking. He'd know. There was no point hoping he wouldn't. It was Charlie. He could probably tell how many glasses she'd had from the taste of her kiss. She let him go, but slowly.

"You're still sober?" she checked.

"You know me and weddings," he answered shyly. The was a faint trace of pink across his cheeks at being kissed in public. God, he was adorable.

She did know him and weddings. She knew him and alcohol, and the way he liked to mix his drinks into solutions that would kill small mammals and leave him dazed for days.

"I got you something," she told him softly. "Just in case you're feeling anxious tonight." Amy took a tiny bottle from the pocket of her dress and pressed it into his hand. She could actually see his eyes light up. "I know Rebecca doesn't approve," she added, "but she doesn't have to know, and it's just a little bit. You're not allowed any more than this. It's doctor's prescription." She kissed his cheek lightly. "Merry Christmas."

"You're very good to me…" Charlie told her softly, returning the gesture and planting a delicate kiss on her cheek as he slipped the bottle into his pocket.

The gentle peck made her feel like she was glowing. However, she couldn't help but notice the indifference with which he'd pocketed the bottle. Her initial instinct went off like a warning siren that he'd already obtained his fix elsewhere, but that was the doctor in her double checking for addicts. Charlie wasn't an addict. At least, he wasn't addicted to any known tangible substance.

"You don't need it…?" she couldn't help but raise the issue just in case.

Charlie shrugged. "Weddings are usually tedious, but I still have the case to occupy me, even if I am presently held up here. Besides… I can't be bored…" He'd gone pink and shy again as he trailed off, but it didn't stop him from softly finding the words. "I have you with me…"

"Charlie?" she smiled at him, feeling a faint heat rise in her own cheeks. "Are you trying to be romantic?"

"Is it working?" he asked.

"Yes," she laughed and kissed his cheek.

Julian was looking rather proud of their little Sleuth as he stood to the side. He had an arm looped casually about Michael, who was watching everyone else entering like he was taking mental notes on all the guests.

"Are we liberating you from your duties or meeting you inside?" Julian asked.

"Meet me inside," Amy answered, kissing Charlie's cheek just one more time. "I'll come find you after the speeches. I should be relatively free after that."

It was sad to see them go, but her duties to the brides came first today. At least, they certainly had to after the way she had failed her responsibilities this morning. Once she was done greeting the arrivals, Amy went back to join her friends.

The two beautiful brides were revelling in the attention. Although, Laura seemed to be enjoying it more than Jane. Laura was practically cackling in glee at the way their mothers were coping with the attendance of an entire High House. No one wanted to make a fuss. It was an honour to have so many beautiful and expensive people in attendance. The fact that Laura's mother and sisters had completely lost control of the situation was just a bonus.

Jane was as subdued as ever. She was quiet and reserved, but there was a softness in her eyes and her smile that betrayed a smitten awe as she basked in her new wife's chaotic joy. Amy understood that feeling. She understood even better the touches of weariness breaking through Jane's amusement, which suggested that while she was enjoying the day, she was very much looking forward to the later, more private, part of the night once everyone else left. Amy found that mindset extremely relatable.

As she thought of Charlie, a commotion began to break out across the garden. She felt her soul sag and began apologising before she even knew what had happened.

"Oh no, darling," Laura kissed her cheek. "Those are some of mine. Your one's over there. He's behaving quite nicely." She pointed and Amy followed her gaze.

Charlie was… behaving. He was sat at a table with Michael and Julian, drinking what looked suspiciously like a cup of tea, and being terribly polite with the catering staff.

"But just in case," Jane murmured quietly, "perhaps you should go check on him."

"Oh, no, I'm sure he's—" Amy began, but her voice faltered under Jane's expression. She blushed and couldn't help but smile. "Thank you," she whispered softly and took the opportunity to dash away.

Her footsteps took her across the garden quickly, but she found herself slowing as she neared the gentlemen at the table. She was not the only one approaching, and the other lady was going to beat her there. She hadn't set out on a rescue mission, but she watched Lady Sterling swoop down on Charlie, and she could see him tense as the old lady's hand latched onto his shoulder like a claw.

"I'm surprised to see you here, Mister Shilling," Lady Sterling's voice carried as Amy neared. "Given the paper this morning, I'd be hiding under my bed if I were you."

Amy felt her corset tighten as she breathed deeply, striding forward and trying to calm herself down from inciting the next incident. She beelined for the old woman and her precious Charlie.

"You know, Mister Shilling, I sent my people down to the printing house first thing!" Sterling declared. "What an atrocity to read over breakfast! I told the editor — I told him! — I said I'm going have him and his staff fired if he takes anymore stories from that vile, money-grubbing shill! Don't you agree, Doctor Florin?"

Amy smiled softly as she reached them. Charlie looked like he'd rather Sterling berate him and sling damning accusations, as the old lady pinched his cheek and turned her attention to Amy.

"This boy is a hero, as I'm sure you can attest, Doctor!" Sterling declared.

"I certainly think so," Amy replied gently, swooping into a rescue after all. Her presence forced Sterling back and gave Charlie some personal space, before she filled the gap and planted a kiss on Charlie's pinched cheek.

"I say we burn the printing house to the ground!" Julian announced. His chair was arranged perfectly beside Michael's so that he could sit sideways and lean back against his husband. Mike didn't seem to mind, although he was eyeing with some apprehension the glass of wine in Julian's hand as his love drunkenly gesticulated. "Think about it — they had their chance. Lionel was already under investigation for fraud and slander before this happened — no one should have been touching his work anyway!"

"Not just under investigation," Mike added, "charged. It's a civil case, for now, but it's in the courts and, after this morning's incident, it could well be escalated to criminal. I wouldn't be surprised. Rumour from London's finest says the only thing keeping Lionel in print is blackmail. I believe there's an investigation into whether it's what's keeping him writing too…"

Amy watched as the boys all shared a look. If she hadn't been paying attention, if she hadn't sobered up somewhat since the gate, she wouldn't have noticed it. Sterling didn't seem to notice. Michael's delivery had an edge to it that suggested he was planting the same seed for the dozenth time. They wanted people to think Tanner was being blackmailed. She tried not to shoot Charlie a look, but her fingers tightened on his shoulder. He took her hand from his coat and kissed her fingers.

"We're not here to speculate," he said. "And, Swift, you are not allowed to set fire to anything. I know you've been drinking, but you promised you'd behave."

"Don't worry, Sleuth," Mike smiled, running the back of a finger along Julian's cheek. "I'll keep him out of trouble."

Julian looked like he was about to jump Michael right there at the table, but they were spared the potentially scandalous development by Lady Sterling's next pronouncement.

"It's almost hard to believe it's taken this long to have the lying worm caught on a hook," the old lady bristled. "Really, the things he's had printed across the years… Your father should have stepped in sooner, Doctor."

"No one ever took Tanner seriously," Amy shrugged. She couldn't seem to keep her hands to herself as she stood by Charlie's chair. Her fingers traced delicately over his shoulders. It was so hard not to mess his hair. It was very smart, properly brushed and set, but it wasn't him. "All of London knows he writes what takes his fancy, regardless of the truth."

Her statement was met with a full house of shaking heads. She pouted.

"*You* know," Michael told her. "Don't make the mistake, Doctor, of thinking everyone is as smart and discerning as you. They're not. Not by a long way. The general population, the ones who are literate anyway, assume that if it's in the paper it has been thoroughly researched and vetted. They assume it's true. That's why half of England thinks you two eloped, why your father took Tanner to court, and why half the city thinks our Sleuth here is a killer. Lies are attractive, and when they masquerade as truth people don't want to know any different. We just have to hope Lord Pound's case goes our way and that the victory of fact over fiction gives people cause to be more discerning for a time."

"Pound will win," Charlie muttered, stroking the rim of his teacup with the side of his thumb and staring at the contents like they were poison.

"Charlie…?" Amy tried to catch his eye and gently touched his cheek.

"Pound will win the case," Charlie repeated, without looking up. "But he'll do it for all the wrong reasons."

"How so, young man?" Sterling inquired, pulling up a chair at the table and watching him curiously.

Amy also pulled up a chair next to her beloved. When sitting, she could see his face and the unhappy pout of his crooked lips. He was practically sullen.

"Go on, Charlie," Michael grinned like he knew what was coming. He placed an arm around Julian who was still leaning against him, as though they were getting comfy for this. "You've been asked, so you're allowed this one. It doesn't count as misbehaving."

"Oh no…" Amy whispered.

Charlie shot her a glance as though miffed. He probably was. It clearly bothered him that she held manners above scruples, but she was a lady, and manners were important. He could do with a few more of his own, quite frankly.

"The justice system is broken," Charlie glowered, his voice cutting and sour. No doubt the extra edge had formed in response to her concern for his attitude. "Lionel deserves to lose because he was lying, but it is very hard to prove. Evidence in a he-said-she-said case is tricky, but Pound is the Lord Chief Justice, so he will make sure the case is won and that Lionel is almost certainly imprisoned." Charlie sighed deeply. "That's not justice, it's vengeance. Lionel's a snake, but he's been after me and other poor victims of circumstance for years. No one stopped him. As you say, Florin, no one ever took him seriously — meaning no one with money ever saw him as a threat. Now, the snake's gone after the wrong man's family. Slander against the daughter of the Lord Chief Justice was stupid, especially when there was real scandal to write. I suppose he wanted something different to the stories everyone else was printing about the Jack, something new to get attention, but he started a fight he can't win. At the end of the day, there is no bigger gang than the aristocracy, and money buys the most power and the harshest weapons. Lionel will get destroyed by a rigged system, and the Lords will all pat themselves on the back that justice has been served. The truth won't even come into it."

"Oh, don't be such a rube, Shilling," Lady Sterling berated him. "The system's working in your favour this time. Have some class, boy, and stop complaining."

Charlie's hands dropped from the cup on the table into his lap, but Amy could see his fists squeezing together with a strength that would have shattered the mug. She could see him willing patience and biting his tongue.

"You know…" Sterling mused disapprovingly, "you remind me of a character from this scandalous new book my daughter had me read recently…"

Amy immediately began to die inside, but at least Charlie was too aggravated to entertain the notion tonight. Not like they hadn't heard it from a dozen people a week since the damn thing had been published. Unfortunately, neither Julian nor Michael had the decency or countenance to play along. Both of them erupted into tears of laughter. Amy glared at them.

"I hope you choke," she told them.

Julian laughed harder, but Mike began to calm himself apologetically. Sterling eyed them all up.

"Oh, you know it then," she sniffed. "Yes, grotesque romanticisation of a man with similar political characteristics to your own — including the ingratitude of your privilege, Mister Shilling."

Julian, bless him, was too drunk to be sensible. Or possibly was just being his normal self.

"*Oooohoohoo*," he chortled. "You know our Sleuth, m'Lady. His rage at an unjust system knows no bounds, and it only gets worse when you mix it with guilt. He's more likely to fight it if he thinks he is getting special treatment."

"There's nothing unjust about our system," Sterling disagreed.

Amy was half in Charlie's lap with her hand over his mouth before she even realised she'd moved. The boys across the table were both laughing at them again, and Sterling had an eyebrow raised. Amy turned her gaze very carefully to Charlie and met his severe eyes above the hand she had pressed to his face. The problem was she knew what he was going to say. She knew everything he was going to say in response and… he wasn't *wrong*. That made it worse. From a moral standpoint, he wasn't wrong in his unsuccessful yet unrelenting battle against the class system that kept Amy and her family in power. But that was the problem. He wanted to upend her entire life and overthrow everything she knew. It was uncomfortable. It was an unpleasant truth that she didn't want to deal with — preferably ever, but particularly tonight. She was trying to keep the wedding civil where she could, and Charlie was looking at her like he was a terrier she was attempting to muzzle and she was either about to be licked or bitten.

"Fight the system, Charlie!" Julian crowed, loud enough to start drawing attention. "Might doesn't make right! Tear down the monarchy!"

Charlie didn't take his eyes from Amy's gaze as an exasperated Michael tried to shush his drunk husband. She couldn't take her eyes from him either, from that cool grey gaze that told her that his affection and respect for her was the only thing buying his silence right now.

"Magdalene, give me patience…" Skipp muttered as he hauled a giggling Julian up and began to drag him off. "Apologies," he told the table. "I think I'd best take this lunatic for a sobering walk. Perhaps away from people, animals, and anything he can find a means to aggravate."

Julian didn't protest as Michael dragged him away. If anything, he seemed to enjoy being manhandled. Amy's surprise proved non-existent. Michael was trying to guide Julian away from civilisation, which Julian took as an invitation to clutch both of Mike's hands and drag him away into the hedge maze. Amy slipped demurely back into her seat beside Charlie, letting her hand fall from his face gently onto his leg. He didn't start anything.

"What a rude man," Lady Sterling sniffed. "Practically treasonous."

"If you think he's bad, you should have met his father…" Charlie commented, carefully picking up his cup and sipping his tea. "Don't worry, I'm sure Skipp's going to pound some sense into him."

"That's unworthy of you, Mister Shilling," Sterling rebuked. "Vulgar though I'm sure his drunken character is, I thought you of all people were opposed to violence—!" She stopped sharply and Amy covered her eyes so that she didn't have to see the expression Charlie was shooting the old lady over the rim of his cup. "Oh, my sweet Lady in Heaven!" Sterling exclaimed. "You didn't mean—! You were—!"

Charlie raised his drink to her, and then drained it in a single gulp, before standing with the intent to excuse himself.

"Good evening, Sterling," he bid her as he headed for the drinks table.

Amy stood and followed him, turning her back quickly so that she didn't have to witness the fallout of the conversation. She kept pace with him to the drinks table and waited until he had handed over his cup for a polite refill before leaning in close and whispering.

"You're a menace," she told him. Charlie looked decidedly unimpressed with the statement and half of her wanted to hear what his response might be in such a mood, but she simply couldn't resist sliding her arms around his neck and adding, "you're a menace, Charlie Shilling, but I do love you terribly."

The tension went out of his face and a small smile escaped, which she took as permission to kiss him, and he gave no objection. He was warm and wonderful on a cold winter's night, with the scent of wood smoke in his hair and firelight in his eyes, even if he couldn't maintain an entire evening of civil conversation with the gentry. That wasn't what she loved about him anyway. She loved him for his kindness and his wit, even when he was being cheeky. At any other time and place, she probably would have found his double entendre funny. It certainly was enough to give one ideas.

"Do you want to follow your friends into the maze…?" she whispered temptingly onto his lips.

"I do not," he replied with amused patience.

"That is a disappointingly reasonable answer," she sighed. He laughed and she felt like she'd won something. She rested her smile against his cheek, holding him close and feeling, despite what the morning had held, like everything might be right with the world for a moment.

It seemed impossible that the other shoe still hadn't dropped. How had things gone so right?

"Charlie…?" she whispered into his ear.

"Mm?" he replied.

"Can I come home with you tonight?" she asked.

"Yes," he whispered, almost like he'd been expecting her to ask. He probably had, knowing him. He followed his response with a kiss on her cheek, before letting her go to retrieve his new cup of tea. She joined him at the drinks table to collect another glass of wine for herself. He had both hands busy with cup and saucer, but Amy tucked her free hand in his elbow as they walked slowly by the fountain, meandering through the flowers.

"Are you mad I didn't let you tell Sterling that you want to abolish the ruling class?" she asked.

"She already knows," Charlie replied. "And it's not about what I want — we need to abolish the ruling class. Society has to learn to govern itself, otherwise it is simply a lottery for who gets to live and who doesn't."

"Work in medicine for a bit, Charlie," Amy told him as gently as she could. "Life is a lottery. Nature doesn't care."

"Capitalism does," Charlie frowned. "Those with money get access to better healthcare, and they have better living conditions to start with. You've been with me to some of the rookeries. Tell me you can look at the slums and not understand that we need to abolish the aristocracy and redistribute the wealth."

"And you think it wouldn't just go on opium and alcohol?" Amy replied.

Charlie's anger flashed with cold ferocity. "That was unworthy of you, Florin. You know better. And I know people with nothing who are more hardworking and resourceful than everyone at this wedding. People like Sterling would tell them they aren't working hard enough, despite working their fingers to the bone every day, would tell them they deserve the conditions of their birth, as though anyone was able to choose such a thing, and the only truth that really matters is that they weren't born in lace doilies."

Amy wanted to tell him no one was born in lace doilies, but she knew what he meant and he was already angry. "It can change," was what she attempted to settle for. "You and Michael both bettered your circumstances."

"We shouldn't have had to," Charlie frowned, his crooked mouth aggravating the expression and the cuteness of it undermining the seriousness of the statement. "Society should look after its weakest members, not leave them in the street, or slums unfit for even rats to live in, while allowing others to call themselves elite for hording wealth and eating off golden plates. It's wrong, Florin. You know it's wrong. Moral corruption at its finest, and every institution with any kind of power, from Parliament to the Crown to the Church, all condone it because it keeps golden plates on their tables." He looked at her with the most earnest gaze imaginable. The kind of look she could feel deep in her chest. "We don't need golden plates, Florin. No one does."

His grey eyes were like cleansing rain, determined to wash away corruption as he saw it, but he made no headway, because they both knew that every time he got worked up about this and made a scene, he usually spent the night in lockup until Rebecca came to get him out. Because, in so many ways, he was right. The rich held the power and they didn't like being told they shouldn't. If he got on his soapbox properly tonight, Laura and Jane wouldn't speak to Amy for a week at least, and Charlie wouldn't do that to her, no matter what he believed. Amy sighed gently and she kissed him. He looked confused.

"I have nothing to add and nothing to argue," she replied. "I just wanted to make you feel better."

"Oh." There was a small pause. "It worked," he admitted, although the reply was rather sullen.

Amy laughed and kissed him again. Then they continued their walk as they sipped their drinks. Their meandering took them back to the brides, who seemed grateful to switch company.

"Shilling!" Laura exclaimed, going in to squeeze him and then taking note of the tea and body language and deciding that perhaps he was better off not being touched. "We've barely seen you all evening, my good man. Where have you been skulking?"

"Not skulking, ma'am," he replied. "At least, not with intent. I've simply been keeping out of the way of the civilised folk."

Amy was endlessly grateful that Laura did not appear to hear the veiled insult in his words, but she wasn't certain Jane hadn't. She hoped she hadn't. If she had, she didn't show it. Her patient eyes watched them and left nothing but mystery across her face. But they all knew Charlie. However much Amy loved him, situations like these were probably why it had taken her so many years to realise he was more than a pest.

"Besides, I understand that this is the way of weddings." Charlie inclined his head politely at the brides and Amy froze in terror, given his general opinion of weddings. Her fear proved unfounded as he elaborated. "Everyone in attendance is here for the two of you, which leaves you stretched rather thin. Sometimes a 'thank you' and 'how do you do' is all there's time for with this many attendees."

"It's starting to feel that way," Laura agreed. "I'm really rather glad we invited everyone from the High House," she laughed. "I feel like it's helping to keep everyone entertained."

"You did tell them not to work tonight... didn't you?" Charlie asked. There was a trace of alarm in his voice that amused Amy.

"They can do what they like as long as they keep Aunt Mildred away from me," Laura commented. "I do not have the patience for a racist tirade tonight, and if what keeps her back is a small legion of escorts, then they deserve to earn a wage."

"Hopefully food and wine will suffice," Jane added. "We're over budget as it is."

"Any relatives you particularly want to alienate, just set Julian on them," Charlie suggested, gesturing carefully with his cup.

Amy turned and saw Julian and Michael sauntering back towards them. They were a strange couple. Her initial impression was always that of Lord and secretary, but the more she watched them the more she could see the small notes of deference in Julian's behaviour, the little glances he shot his husband in the wake of every action, as though constantly seeking approval or amusement. Michael always walked a half-step behind Julian, but it wasn't a mark of respect, more an act of caution, as though making sure he could always watch out for his troublemaker.

"I see you managed to keep him from causing a scene," Julian praised Amy, as he swept over to them in a gale of bright colours and perfume.

"No thanks to you," she preened, secretly delighting in his smirk. "How was the maze?" she opened the question to Michael as well, almost as though she hoped to keep things civil, but knowing full well she was tempting fate.

"Prickly," Julian answered.

Charlie snorted into his tea. Michael glowered at him, but his face strained desperately to maintain the disapproval without giving way to hilarity.

"That explains the grass stains..." Jane commented.

"Well, don't tell everyone," Julian smirked. "They'll all want some, and I don't share him."

Michael was scarlet by this point and looked very much like he wanted to hide behind Charlie. Unfortunately, Charlie was the shortest of all of them and wasn't much use in the shield department. He was also sipping his tea in an attempt to hide his amusement. Michael's recovery was composed in everything but the colour of his cheeks, and his tone calm, even suggestive, as he cocked an eyebrow like he wasn't the shade of a glowing sunrise.

"And where, might we suppose, are your grass stains, ladies?" he inquired. "It is your wedding, after all."

"You know, he makes an excellent point," Amy agreed, sipping her wine.

"That is an excellent point," Laura agreed suggestively.

"Absolutely not," Jane stated.

"But it's your wedding!" Amy declared, raising her voice enough to start pulling the attention of nearby guests. "You simply must! I'm sure there's plenty of people here who would be more than happy to supervise."

"Oh my goodness!" Laura exclaimed. "Like they used to do in France! I've never had an audience before."

"Absolutely. Not." There was a genuine note of panic in Jane's voice as she realised her flirtatious bride was taking the idea seriously.

"We'll give you a ten second head start," Amy

promised, carefully prying the wineglass from Jane's hand and smirking mischievously at her. She set Jane's glass on the nearby bridal table for her return. "Ten!"

Laura was laughing as she grabbed her new wife's hand and dashed towards the maze entrance. Jane was still protesting, but the objections fell on deaf ears, and she hitched her skirts carefully as she was dragged away at speed.

"Nine!" Amy called after them, slowly starting forward. She continued her countdown, sauntering at a glacial pace and feeling the others start to gather and follow behind her. Her count of 'one' brought her to entrance of the maze and she made sure she was yelling loud enough for her friends to hear. "Ready or not!" she cried. Then stopped and downed her entire glass, or what was left of it. She turned around and found a more sizable crowd than expected behind her, although it was possible some were just curious as to what was occurring. "Oh no," she laughed. "Back to the wine, you degenerates. There's nothing to see here." She raised both hands, one with the empty glass still in her fingers, and carefully ushered the crowd away, chuckling at the confusion and in some cases possible disappointment.

She noted that Charlie and Michael had not followed and were waiting patiently where she had left them. Julian, unsurprisingly, was at her side.

"You're an excellent Maid of Honour," he praised, pulling her in with one arm and kissing her cheek.

"I am an excellent Maid of Honour," she agreed, holding her glass out for a refill as one of the servers went by. They topped her up and Julian escorted her back.

"Sleuth," Julian addressed Charlie as they returned, "she's magnificent. How come you haven't asked her to marry you yet?"

Amy closed her eyes in sympathy as she watched Charlie choke rather painfully on his tea. Mike patted him on the back and Amy waited until it looked like he could mostly breathe again before answering on his behalf.

"Probably because he knows that after an entire lifetime of being betrothed I'm rather relishing the freedom," she supplied.

"And here I assumed it was because he loathes weddings," Julian grinned. "I'm honestly surprised we got you here tonight, Sleuth."

"It's true," Michael gave them a small smile. "That he'll put aside a case to come to a wedding with you, Doctor, says more than any 'I do' ever could."

Amy watched them talk up her beloved as he slowly caught his breath again. They were trying to praise him, to sell her on his character, as though she needed it. There was something about what they said though. Something about their tones, the look in their eyes…

"You arses are working," she accused them.

All three of them instantly protested, their objections falling thick and fast and tripping over each other. Amy gave them a long, judgemental stare.

"Bastards," she cursed them, turning away. In truth, she was mostly angry at herself for not having realised sooner. Of course they were working. Charlie didn't know how to do anything else. It was possible he physically couldn't bring himself to pause a case for anything other than the occasional rest and sustenance it took to keep him functioning.

"Amy…" He was at her side quickly, gaze imploring, and she did her best to shut him down with a look.

"Darling, I'm going to be cross with you for a bit," she warned him. "I'm probably going to go and complain, quite fairly, to Lizzie and Bronny about you until Jane manages to drag Laura back out of the maze. Then I'm going to spend the rest of the evening with my newly wedded friends until it's time to leave. I imagine that somewhere in those next hours I will forgive you, but you'll have to let me gripe first."

Charlie looked at her with such adoration that she nearly forgave him on the spot, but that would set a terrible precedent, so she steeled herself against his adorable face and turned her back on him sternly. He let her walk away with nothing but admiration, which made going to complain to the ladies about him rather difficult, but she did her best anyway.

In the end, she didn't speak to the gentlemen again until it was time to leave. Laura and Jane did return after not particularly long and with a disappointing lack of grass stains, but at least they were in good humour about it. She had always been able to count on her friends to share her jokes.

The night had probably progressed to early morning, but had not yet worn thin, when she piled herself into a carriage with Charlie and his friends to head home. Julian looked like he was having an excellent time, Michael looked like he was in desperate need of somewhere quiet to think, and Charlie… Charlie looked tired. Charlie looked like he was trying not the carry the weight of the world as he dealt with more death, more guilt, and more socialising than his personality could handle. He was twisting his ring in bold, circular movements as he sat beside her and they trundled back towards town.

"So, are we dropping you anywhere on the way, Doctor?" Mike asked.

"No," she smiled and planted a soft kiss on Charlie's temple. "I'm over my disapproval now."

"I'm surprised you cared in the first place," Julian commented, sprawled across Michael in a lazy and drunken repose. "You want this bastard caught as badly as the rest of us."

"I do," she agreed. "I think part of me hoped that at least one thing could be kept sacred, that my best friends' wedding would be safe, but I suppose I can't blame you."

"Eh, waste of a good irritation, honestly," Julian lamented. "Deadbeats and dead ends everywhere."

"We don't know that," Michael countered, gently stroking Julian's hair as he sat nestled into the corner with his husband lying on him. "All we did tonight was sow the seeds. We have to wait and see if any of them germinate."

"So what were you troublemakers up to?" Amy inquired.

Charlie stopped stimming his ring and dug into his pocket to produce his notebook, which he flipped to a smudged sketch of a symbol she recognised.

"That's the emblem of one of Harry's old clubs," she commented.

All three of them nodded at her. Charlie quickly explained where he had found it and the context of what they had been trying to do.

"Julian's a bit right though," he finished lamely. "There weren't nearly as many members of LOAM there as I'd anticipated, which was perhaps shortsighted of me, given the brides."

"What's LOAM?" Amy asked. "That's not a club I've heard of before."

Michael and Julian chuckled.

"It's the acronym we came up with for the less desirable collective of Harry's old associates," Charlie admitted. "The ones that would attempt to defend his actions and are, quite frankly, the dirt of our species."

"It stands for League Of Aristocratic Misogynists," Mike smirked.

"I know the ones you're talking about," Amy nodded. "That's quite clever."

"It makes it easier to talk about them in public," Julian added. "Especially when we're starting to think one of them might be pulling the strings on Lionel."

"And that's what we think now?" Amy asked.

The boys all looked between each other, sharing nods and shrugs. She watched them in the dim light of the carriage and pondered.

"You should have called them LOAN," she commented. They all looked at her curiously. "Half of them are bankers and, while I appreciate where your sentiment comes from, if you wanted to accurately summarise the lot of them, it would be more precise to label them League Of Aristocratic Narcissists."

Her statement was met with general chuckles.

"Both things can be true," Charlie sighed. "I know there are still pieces of this that I'm missing, but Lionel has ties to a club he shouldn't have access to, and someone is manipulating him. LOAM, or LOAN, would have the power to do that, have known sympathies for Harry and the Jack, and they *hate* me."

Amy reached out a hand almost unconsciously to stroke his hair behind his ear. The messy straw stack had slowly been returning to form over the evening, and she felt compelled to straighten it, and even more compelled to soothe him from the emphasis of loathing he put into his description of LOAM's opinion of him. He wasn't wrong, but she wished he was.

"So, first things first," Michael began, "you two promise me you'll get some sleep tonight."

"After I'm done with him," Amy promised smugly. Julian laughed.

"I'll keep an ear out for any movement on the threads we're following," Mike promised in return. "Your first job for tomorrow, after a decent rest, is to investigate Smoke & Arrow."

"And let me know if you need help," Julian insisted.

"I will," Charlie nodded. "For now, Swift, I want to keep you in my back pocket."

Julian made a suggestive sound and Michael bopped him admonishingly on the head.

"Yes," Charlie sighed wearily. "I'm going to need

you significantly more sober before I try and bring you in on any kind of plan."

"I'm much more useful inebriated," Julian declared passionately, tipping his head back to gaze lovingly at Michael and reaching up a hand to stroke his cheek.

"You're an idiot," Mike smiled affectionately and kissed his forehead.

Julian didn't argue, and he didn't push to have Charlie let him in on any plans. They travelled back to Kensington under quiet nightfall, with serious discussions regarding the severity of the case and the uncomfortably large pool of current suspects.

7

The next morning was dark and cold. Charlie didn't even have to look outside to know it was finally here, the first snow of the season. The fire in the hearth was warm and crackling. Someone had kindly lit it last night while they were out and Charlie had added fresh logs before bed.

He hadn't slept much. It had been late when he got home. No, early. The day had taken its toll and he'd needed to sleep... until Amy had convinced him otherwise. She could be terribly persuasive when she wanted to be. In the end, he'd slept for perhaps a few hours and woken to the crackling fire, and his churning brain's insistence that he had rested enough. But Amy was asleep on his chest and he didn't want to wake her, so he lay in the bed and watched the flames dance in the hearth as he delicately played with her curls.

He knew something was wrong the instant he heard the knock at the door. There were a million reasons for someone to be knocking at the door, but Charlie knew it concerned him as soon as he heard it. It wasn't even vanity, just honesty. Maybe he was used to picking up distinct knocking patterns. He knew it was the police.

He tried to get himself up gently without disturbing

Amy, and he nearly made it, but she caught him slipping from the bed. By then, he could hear muffled voices at the front door.

"Charlie…?" she snuffled sleepily, peering at him blurry-eyed from a nest of auburn curls.

"Go back to sleep," he advised, kissing her cheek.

She ignored him, seemingly catching on instantly to what was happening. He wasn't sure how long the officers were held at the door, but both he and Amy were up and dressed by the time the knock came at their door.

Jasper was on the other side.

"Sorry to disturb you, Sir—" he began.

Charlie met his eye. Jasper tried so hard never to do that anymore, but he allowed this one. He let Charlie know things were grim with a simple look. Wilson and Bond were on the landing behind him. Charlie looked over all of them with all the energy he could muster and hoped he wasn't coming up short.

"Who died?" he asked.

Charlie couldn't even say he was surprised. He wanted to be surprised, but it was far more surprising that Jasper took the coach out to drive them there. Charlie had refused to wake Ruth, their usual coach driver, after keeping her out all night, and Jasper had refused to let Charlie be seen getting into a police wagon. Everyone had bundled into the carriage and Jasper had driven them to the crime scene.

He hadn't been wrong. There was a light dusting of snow out and it blanketed the world like it could hide away all sins. According to Wilson and Bond, Detective Rupee wanted to see him. Remembering the detective as he did, Charlie was very confident that 'want' was not the right word. Rupee wouldn't 'want' to see him if they were the last two people on earth. But if someone was dead, perhaps found with their throat slit and their heart cut out over their typewriter, and 'Shilling' scrawled in blood across the wall, then perhaps Rupee might feel a pressing 'need' to see him.

Charlie wrapped his scarf around the lower part of his face and held the collar of his jacket up across the rest, shielding himself selfishly from the flashing lights of the clustered reporters gathered outside the cordon. The papers had never managed to get a photo of him investigating a crime scene and he'd be damned if they were going to start now.

The cold made him want to put a protective arm around Amy, but she was bundled in her own coats and he didn't want to give anyone something to photograph, or to gossip about. There were a group of carollers singing across the road. He wanted to give them the benefit of the doubt that they weren't rubbernecking, but he didn't trust humans that much. Also, the solemn hymns made the situation feel worse, as though a choir wanted to remind them God was present. Not for this she wasn't.

The apartment was almost the same as it had been yesterday, save for all the uniforms and all the blood.

Save for Lionel being very gruesomely dead. Detective Rupee, as Shilling remembered her, was a short woman with a round face and it had never in all the years he'd known it been happy to see him. Today was no exception. He stepped inside the room with Florin at his side and Wilson and Bond flanking them like an honour guard. Or like jailors. Jasper, bless him, had opted to wait with the carriage.

"Shilling…" Rupee greeted him, barely supressing a sneer at the sight of him.

"Detective," Charlie nodded politely, clutching the lapels of his pale, ragged coat as he looked around.

"And Doctor Florin," Rupee's voice softened instantly. "It's a pleasure to meet your ladyship."

"Detective," Amy reached out and shook the other woman's hand.

"So, I see the rumours are true after all," Rupee eyeballed them. "You two do come as a joint pair these days."

"I thought it best to accompany Mister Shilling this morning as we paid a joint visit here yesterday," Amy replied carefully.

"Did you now?" Rupee cocked an eyebrow.

"You already know that, Detective," Charlie told her, carefully casting his eye over the room. "The landlady already told you."

Rupee was glaring at him like he was being annoying, but so far all he'd done was exist, and perhaps save them a bit of time with tedious and unnecessary questioning.

"Can you tell me what happened?" Charlie asked,

hoping to focus on the work rather than the unpleasantness.

"Aren't you supposed to be the—" Rupee began.

"Don't patronise me, Detective," Charlie cut her off. "I can see the situation very clearly for myself. However, I have been summoned for consultation *by you*. Not an event either of us expected. I am not meeting you at the station to be interrogated. I am not under arrest, yet. You invited me to the crime scene. Why?"

Rupee rolled her eyes at him, but her gaze finished on the wall and his own followed it to the large smears of blood that spelt out his name.

"I want to know what's going on, Shilling," Rupee replied. "I want to know who's doing this to my city and how it involves you. Why is there a copycat? If this is how they feel, why didn't they just save us all some time and start with you?"

"'Cause he's wily and notoriously hard to kill, Ma'am," Wilson muttered.

Charlie saw Amy and Bond share a smile out of the corner of his eye. He rubbed his mouth in thought. From this distance, it looked like Lionel had been killed by the same copycat. There were discolorations that suggested he had still been drugged when his attacker had struck, and no sign of defensive wounds. Interesting, given that Charlie had stolen the obvious stash of drugs.

"I apologise, Detective," Charlie began, "for any previous degradations insinuated to your skill."

"Oh, don't be a prick, Shilling," Rupee snorted,

folding her arms and glaring at him. "We both worked the Jack case and, smartest man alive, it took you more than a year to crack as well, so don't pretend like you ever really thought I was bad at my job. No one expected it to be the Lord Chief Justice's son. Not even you." She shot Amy a look. "I'd say sorry for your loss, Doctor, if I thought for an instant you were."

Charlie drew himself up immediately, which would probably have meant more if he wasn't also so short. He wouldn't have had much height on Rupee, if any, and the scathing amusement in her eyes told him as much. His indignation was short lived, however, not by his failure at intimidation, but by Amy's obvious amusement.

"I can see why you two don't like each other," she commented.

"'Cause he's a vigilante at best, a crook at worst, a pain in everyone's arse, and he keeps sticking his nose where it don't belong?" Rupee muttered. "He's easy not to like, Doctor. Coulda been one of the best of us, but Shilling here don't like the law, don't respect it, and won't play by the rules. Won't wear the uniform. Thinks he's better than us. Well, Charlie-boy, this is what happens when you pick fights and play at being a hero — you get people killed." She pointed at the wall. "This is a warning to you. Someone wants your attention."

"They have it," Charlie assured.

"Or the reporter owed a guy money?" Bond shrugged hypothetically. "Though it seems a small amount to kill someone over."

Wilson nodded supportively while Charlie pinched

his brow to keep from despairing. Those two actually made him glad Rupee was in charge. The detective was ignoring the constables, and the only distraction was the camera flash of the scene photographer finishing up their work.

"All clear, Detective," they announced, carefully packing away their camera equipment. "I think that's everything. You want me to send in the coroner?"

"Please," Rupee nodded. "Thank you, Hobbs."

Amy stepped forward as Hobbs gave a polite nod and finished packing up.

"If you need any help—" she began.

"No thank you, Doctor," Rupee cut her off dismissively. "I appreciate your skillset, and I know your associations usually get you and Shilling whatever access you'd like, but we're doing this one by the book. I cannot, for an instant, pretend that the two of you aren't connected to this case — I just don't know how yet. So we're going to talk, you're going to have a look and tell me what you think, and you're not going to touch anything or I'm going to book the both of you and live with the consequences." Rupee met their eyes with an unrelenting stubbornness. "By all accounts, Doctor, I hear your father is a reasonable man, and I am doing my job."

Charlie glanced at Amy. She met his eye. They both knew better than to fight this. This was trouble of the highest order. They needed to tread carefully. Unfortunately, more trouble was finding them. He should have known. He did know, half a second before it burst over him, the shrill sound of panic and disgust.

"What the shit is he doing here?!" Monty screamed the instant she was in the doorway.

"How does London not have more than one coroner?" Amy demanded, turning to face Monty.

"Or more than two uniformed officers," Charlie added, casting a direct look at Wilson and Bond and deliberately ignoring all the other uniformed officers at the scene.

"Monty, do us a favour, and keep it civil," Rupee sighed.

"He's a killer, Rupee!" Monty yelled from the doorway, almost like she wanted people to hear. Her stance refused to move over the threshold. "He's *the* killer! The landlady heard Tanner yelling yesterday that Shilling was going to kill him! His name's on the bloody wall!"

Rupee pinched the bridge of her nose like she was willing patience, and her response came pained and frustrated.

"Look, I'm not a medical expert, but last I checked it's not possible to write things out in your own blood *after* your heart has been cut from your body," she stated.

"It would also be impossible for Lionel to have made those marks without leaving some spray once his throat had been slit," Amy added. "Which, from the looks of things, was the first injury he sustained. You can see from the blood spray that, just like Sarah, he was attacked from behind, had his throat cut, was pinned while he bled, and then his body was turned so that they could cut out his heart. It's the same butcher too, the cuts are more hacked than sliced." She paused and glanced at Rupee. "Apologies, I know you weren't looking for my medical opinion."

Rupee looked like she wanted to kick them all from the room, but she'd asked them to come and now she had to live with the consequences.

"It makes you wonder if perhaps the killer hasn't been taking care of the knife they stole..." Charlie mused. "Harry kept excellent care of his blade and it was precision sharp. Perhaps his wannabe doesn't have the knowledge... or, far more interestingly, the inclination?"

"You'd know," Monty spat.

"He's alibied for the murders, Monty!" Rupee snapped aggressively. "You think that isn't the first goddamn thing we checked?! Get in here and do your bloody job, you twat."

"How can you defend him?!" Monty demanded.

"Because I don't have to like him to understand that he's on our side," Rupee answered. "I ran a profile on him when I was investigating the Jack. He was top of my list then, even with the number of alibis he had. The Jack was a ruthless and calculated killer. Having Shilling fit that bill wasn't a stretch. This isn't the same killer. We all know that, Mont. Stop being such a twat about it."

Monty did not look happy and refused to budge into the room.

"How'd you already know I was alibied?" Charlie asked.

"You were at a wedding with hundreds of witnesses,

Shilling," Rupee snorted. "Word gets about, don't it?"

"It would have been easy to sneak out—" Monty began.

"Monty, shut the hell up," Rupee snapped. "Your damnation of him only serves to doubt my competency. If you've got a problem with my work, take it up with my Captain. He was halfway out of London until three in the morning — at least an hour each way plus time for the murder, and he wasn't ever without company for that long. Multiple witnesses have already come forward. Lionel's death was reported just after midnight. Someone heard the screams about ten past twelve. Body was found before one. It cannot have been Shilling. There's simply no way."

"Witnesses?" Charlie cocked an eyebrow.

Rupee sneered at him. "Apparently one of your people was having this idiot watched. Kids peeping on him said they heard screams and saw a ghost, reported it to us, but I imagine they reported it to your man at the same time."

"Hm, not that I knew about," Charlie admitted, processing quickly. Michael had been with him all evening, mostly, and there hadn't been any communications to him last night. Everything ran to the bakery, so one of the other Pences would have collected everything for when he returned. Still, he hadn't sent any messages over. Julian might not have given him time to go through everything. Charlie doubted anything was delivered while Mike had been hiding in the maze.

"Honestly, Shilling, it sounds like you had an

uncharacteristically busy evening," Rupee commented. "Almost like you knew you'd need an alibi… not that I'm suggesting anything."

Charlie glanced at Amy and the two of them shared a long look. They both knew how close he had been to skipping the wedding yesterday. If he'd done that, would he be staring at the inside of a jail cell right now? Someone was trying to set him up. Someone who must have been keeping tabs on him. But it didn't make any sense. If they wanted him set up, why write his name on the wall? If they wanted his attention, why not leave a letter?

Charlie breathed deep and slow as he tried to make sense of it, inhaling the unhealthy mix of scents that the crime scene had to offer.

"Detective," he addressed Rupee. "You said there were children who saw something? They saw a ghost and heard screams before running?"

"Kids were hysterical," Rupee shrugged. "And you know the imaginations of urchins."

"Where was the ghost?" Charlie asked.

"You have got to be shitting me, Shilling," Rupee scoffed. "I know you don't believe in that tripe."

"Was it in the garden?" Charlie asked. "Out the window? Looking in? Just the way Lionel said it was yesterday?"

"Hey, now," Bond raised both her hands defensively, "no one said anything about this place being haunted."

"It should comfort you to know, Constable, that no ghosts were ever actually seen in the building, I believe," Charlie deduced. "Detective, I need to go and check the garden. Would you like to accompany me and I can show you what I found there yesterday? Perhaps we can leave Monty the room to do her job."

"Not a bad idea," Rupee nodded grudgingly. "Coming, Doctor?"

"If no one minds," Amy began carefully, "my area of expertise lies in here. Perhaps I can stay and assist our coroner, should they require any aid."

No one argued and indifferent shrugs were shared around. As deeply as Monty loathed Shilling, she didn't seem to harbour any particular ill-will to Florin. Charlie touched Amy's arm briefly as he passed, although which of them he was reassuring with the gesture was anyone's guess. She gave him a nod in return, almost a half-smile, although this didn't seem the time or place for smiles. He led Rupee outside to the garden and let Monty have the room.

8

Monty only waited a second for Charlie to be gone before moving in to set up. Amy tried her best to be casual in her loitering, but she knew Monty was as aware of her as she was of the coroner. There was a deep part of her, a naturally suspicious and betrayed part of her, that wanted to make sure Monty wasn't about to tamper with the body. The fixation with which Monty seemed to despise Charlie gave Amy cause to consider that there might genuinely be something nefarious afoot. If the people responsible had gotten to Lionel, they could have gotten to Monty too. It wouldn't have been hard. For all Amy knew, Monty would help frame Charlie for free. They wouldn't even need blackmail.

And yet… as Amy watched her work, Monty didn't do anything she wouldn't have done herself. Monty took care and pride in her examination. No signs of foul play in the investigation so far. She looked to be doing a better job now than what Amy had seen the first day in the morgue, back when she had first agreed to help Charlie get a second opinion on the Jack of Hearts murders.

"I get it, you know," Monty muttered, not taking her eyes from her grizzly inspection. "I get why you can't bear for it to be him."

"Monty…" Amy sighed wearily, not in the mood for this conversation again.

"No, I get it," Monty insisted. "You think Harry killed those women. You think Shilling rescued you from him, that's why you're settling for him and why you can't bear the thought that he might be the real killer — that he's stolen everything from you — it makes perfect sense, Florin. It really does… but how many bodies does the man have to be tied to before you admit he's the problem? This isn't even the first body with his name on it this year! We both know that he's the person who stole the journal from evidence. It makes sense that he stole the knife too. It makes sense that he's back to his old tricks and trying to cover it up."

"Monty," Amy said with all the patience she could muster, "if Charlie didn't exist, if he was not here and had never been involved in these cases, would you really think these new deaths were committed by the original Jack?"

Monty flushed angrily and didn't look at her.

"I know you liked Harry," Amy whispered, trying not to remember how much she'd loved him herself. "I know that he was handsome in a way that made people warm to him. I'm sure he was kind to you, in a world of snobbery that probably looks down on your station and your work. Harry was a narcissist who liked it when people liked him — liked it when people needed him. Monty, Harry kept a trunk in his office that turned out to be full of glass jars that contained formaldehyde and human hearts. Hearts that he cut out of women who he made wear my perfume before he paid them for sex and slaughtered them."

"But he was set up!" Monty insisted. "Harry would never have done that! The boys all know he was framed! It's not your fault, Florin. It's not your fault you were tricked, but you need to admit that you're a victim of Shilling's malicious scheme or you'll never get away from it!"

"There was no set up, Monty," Amy shook her head. "I helped to investigate. I caught Harry. Yes, Shilling was there when Harry was finally arrested. Yes, the papers all say he caught the Jack. But I worked it out first. I caught Harry. No one was framed. The man I'd been betrothed to my whole life, the man I loved and called family, the man I was supposed to marry, was killing women. I caught him doing it. I told Charlie, and he helped me bring him to justice. I understand why Harry's friends want to deny it. I understand why you want to, but doubling down on this foolishness just because your friends want you to believe it, when you are quite literally staring at evidence to the contrary, isn't just stupid. It's cruel and selfish. The dead deserve better. They deserve actual justice based on facts, not the personality of their investigators."

Monty looked like she was going to argue, but Amy wasn't done.

"And Monty," she stated with so much venom the coroner flinched, "I am many things, many sometimes wonderful and sometimes regrettable things, but I am no one's victim. I am not the victim of a mother who abandoned me, nor a victim of a fiancé who betrayed me. I am certainly not the victim of the delusions of a room of narcissistic and misogynistic little boys."

"Only your own delusions, then," Monty sighed as though witnessing a great tragedy. "You don't have to like me, Florin, you can belittle my friends if it makes you feel better about what you did to Harry, but you're a smart woman — do you really think anyone would believe you if you tried to tell them that Shilling having his name carved into a little girl and then scrawled in blood above another body less than six months later was normal?"

"Nothing about Charlie is normal," Amy admitted. "And I would never try and pretend it was. But..." she paused in thought for a moment as the realisation hit her. "But... the constant onslaught of attacks on him by the cruel and homicidal tells me he must be doing something right. If the people who don't like him, who want to hurt him, are the worst of humanity then he must be an agent of good. I know that people like you, and the LOAM boys, and Tanner have been working endlessly to bring him down and sour opinions of him, but you're not winning. You cannot make a villain of that man, Monty. No one can. Not even Kopeck, and she killed a child to try and break him."

There was a ringing silence at the end of her declaration that made Amy feel for a moment that she might finally have gotten through to the other woman, but then Monty breathed a noise that sounded far too much like a chuckle.

"You know..." Monty began softly, "if you're right... if Shilling's just a good guy trying his best in a world of thieves and killers, then that means he's the most unlucky bastard in London. Death is following him, Doctor. It already tried to take you once in his company. Best be sure it's not going to catch you again."

Charlie took Rupee outside, dodging carefully around the side of the building to avoid the reporters. The singing was louder out here. Too loud to ignore. The trees did nothing to block the ghostly choir, and the snow wasn't deep enough to dampen it. He paused at the start of the path, eyeing the snow — the pattern and fall of it. He was grateful it was thin, even more grateful it was disturbed. A fresh dusting hid some of it, but the way it clumped betrayed last night's activity.

Charlie was agonisingly careful as he showed Rupee where he'd seen the markings in the earth yesterday, as well as the pale fibres and paint. Sure enough, there was more. Fresh everything. Some of the ornaments had even been knocked from the branches last night by someone scuffling around back here. The white in the trees was almost disguised by snow, but Rupee was good at her job. She might not have known what to look for, but she knew how to recognise it when it was pointed out to her. He ran her through his theory on someone using the Pepper's Ghost illusion to trick witnesses into thinking Lionel was haunted — or at least had been seeing a legitimate spectre.

"So, that's the answer," Rupee frowned. "A wizard

did it."

"A magician," Charlie corrected. "There's no actual magic involved, Detective. Just light and shadow, smoke and mirrors."

"I know, kid," Rupee sighed. "I get it." She breathed into her gloved hands to warm them as she looked around. "Do you know how long these... 'hauntings' were going on?"

Charlie shook his head. "Lionel was high as a kite yesterday and he hates me. I know it was the last two nights minimum, but it could have been going on much longer. We will need to canvas to find out if anyone else knows anything or if they ever saw what was happening down here, but it was clearly a very particular trick, in a very specific place, for a very narrow audience."

Rupee nodded in agreement. "Mister Tanner got himself visited by the ghosts of Christmas Past, Present, and Future... and it looks like the wrong one caught up with him," she mused to herself. The detective crouched down to inspect the markings carefully, meticulous not to touch anything and to avoid leaving more footprints on the pavers than she had to. "Glass is heavy, and these markings look like whoever did this was using large sheets."

"Indeed," Charlie nodded.

Rupee looked up at him with deep foreboding. "Shilling, it's one thing to say there's a copycat Jack who's killing... who's killed two people in just two days... that's quite the peak horror story on its own... but this..."

"Is a conspiracy…" Charlie sighed, knowing Rupee and every official member of law enforcement would hate it.

"You would need at least two strong men to move the pieces for this trick," Rupee muttered under her breath, standing again so that she could speak only to him and wouldn't risk anyone else overhearing. "At a bare minimum that means two people involved in this, and I get the impression that you think more."

"It is possible," Charlie mused, burying his cold lips in his scarf, "that the people involved in the ghost trick and the killer are separate. I have neither seen nor heard of any evidence to suggest ghosts or illusions played a part in the death of Sarah Tuppence."

"So, if we're lucky then — *if we're really bloody lucky* — some arseholes were blackmailing our reporter friend," Rupee posed. "Maybe trying to spook him a bit, maybe put something is his drink to make him a bit paranoid, and maybe… those pricks saw who killed him. Maybe they weren't all in on the same thing, and maybe they bolted like startled rats…" She gestured at the mess of snapped twigs, fallen ornaments, and traces of ghost. "But maybe we can find them too."

"These tracks…" Charlie mused, insomuch as he could even call the old lumps in the snow tracks, painfully aware that the most obvious marks now were caused by them and that it was unavoidable. "They seem to lead back into the building. Or they come from the building…?"

"You think it's someone here then?" Rupee checked. "Makes sense, actually. Think about it, the pieces they'd need to set up an illusion that big here… you'd want to keep them right there in the building…"

Charlie shared a look with the detective and then they both moved as one, dashing back inside. Charlie nearly forgot to hold his collar over his face as he heard the clamour of reporters and the sudden flash of a camera. Would those vultures never find anything better to do?! They couldn't even get a decent image from back on the cordon line, but still they persevered. He supposed he should admire their tenacity.

Rupee beat him back into the building, but he stayed hot on her heels. She immediately sent one of her officers upstairs to fetch the landlady back down. They had a few more questions, probably of the replacing windows variety. Charlie was too impatient to wait. Besides, relying on a person to tell the truth to solve a case was a fast recipe for nothing.

He stalked the hallway, keen of eye and sharp of ear. Sharper even of nose, despite the overpowering stench of pine. Traces of mud showed on the carpet near one particular doorway. Charlie knelt down to scratch and sniff at the dried mud. It led from the front door and it was most definitely the same mud from the garden. A smooth even line of it, almost as though it had come off the corner of a mirror — a heavy one someone had set down, just for a moment.

It stood to reason, by the same logic that suggested storing the glass in the apartment building was the most sensible move, that storing it in one of the ground floor apartments was the most likely option. As long as the culprits had the money or influence to make that happen. Charlie was presently confident that they did.

"Rupee," Charlie motioned to her. She looked irritated at being summoned, but he was being helpful. He pointed out the mud to her. She looked at him like she couldn't tell different kinds of mud apart, which was preposterous — colour, texture, sediment, smell... the earth had more variation than people.

Before he had time to let his frustration show, and before she had time to pick a fight with him, the landlady was brought to see them. Charlie recognised her from yesterday, but today she clutched a tearstained handkerchief to her face and her eyes were red and puffy.

"Sorry to trouble you again, ma'am," Rupee began. "We just have a few more questions—"

"What do you keep behind this door?" Charlie asked. He barely registered Rupee's glare as he scoured the landlady's face for clues. Her expression conveyed mostly confusion.

"T-that's one of the apartments I let," she stammered tearfully.

"Who lives there?" Charlie demanded.

"N-no one at t-the moment," she replied. "It was Mister Baker's room, but he moved out a week ago. I-I haven't filled it yet."

"Shilling..." Rupee pinched the bridge of her nose exasperatedly as Charlie knelt down to inspect the lock.

"No one else uses this room?" he checked.

"No one," the landlady shook her head. "Mister Baker gave back the keys when he left, and I have the only other set. My tenants have a right to their privacy!"

she defended.

Charlie nodded approvingly. "There's no sign that anyone picked this lock."

"You mean before you?" Rupee muttered.

Charlie stood up and raised his hands, backing away. "Unnecessary, Detective. It's a very basic lock and would be easy to pick, but no one seems to have bothered, and if our kind host can let us in, I see no reason for that to change."

The two women shared a look, and the landlady began delicately flicking through the ring of keys on her apron. Rupee was looking at Charlie again with pointed sarcasm.

"You really don't see the irony, do you, Shilling?" she muttered. "In all the laws you break trying to catch other people breaking laws."

"I successfully catch others, Detective," Charlie pointed out. "And don't pretend like you and yours don't do exactly the same thing. At least I'm uncovering evidence, not planting it."

Rupee looked like she was about to arrest him for stating an unpleasant truth, though he wasn't sure what the actual charges would be. Fortunately, they were both saved the discovery by the landlady who stepped forward with the key and unlocked the room.

It was a plain space with simple furnishings. One wardrobe, one desk and chair, one single bed — stripped and awaiting fresh linen. Lace curtains offered some privacy from the garden outside, but otherwise the curtains stood open and daylight, dim and shaded by the trees, lit the room.

The first thing Charlie noticed was the mud on the floor, and he wasn't the only one. The landlady was instantly tutting at the mess she didn't realise had been left here. Charlie scoured the obvious in an instant. This was the room the pieces of the magic trick had been kept in. Emphasis on *had*. They were no longer there, although there were marks on the floor and wall to show where they had been. There were at least two sets of distinct footprints. It was the windowsill he moved to first though.

While Rupee investigated the marks on the floor and took measurements, Charlie checked the window. Unlocked, but not obviously so. Anyone who knew about it could come and go as they pleased. In fact, there were flakes of white paint on the sill. This was almost certainly how the 'ghost' had come and gone and where the magician had based their trick from.

He filled Rupee in on his discovery, before turning to the shocked landlady.

"I need to know everything you do about this Mister Baker," he insisted.

She stood and stared at him a moment with her mouth agape, but recovered herself before he was forced to coax a response.

"I... I don't know that much about him," she admitted bashfully, unhelpfully describing a very ordinary brunette man with no distinctive features. "I hardly think he would be involved in something like this though! He was always polite, but quiet, and he paid his rent on time. Never any trouble, Mister Baker. He was a gentleman, just a touch shy."

"Someone knew this room was empty, and someone left the window unlocked," Charlie pointed out. "You didn't seem to know about it."

"Well, I didn't!" she huffed.

"That leaves Mister Baker as the last occupant," Charlie deduced. "How long did he live here?"

"Only two months," the landlady sniffed. "I try to get good, reliable, long-term tenants here, where possible. I thought I'd found that in Mister Baker too, but he said his circumstances changed and had to leave early. No hard feelings, though. He was very good about paying out the last month of his lease. That's why I hadn't been quite so desperate to fill the room."

"Any disagreements between him and Lionel?" Charlie asked.

The colour drained from the woman's face and she shook her head, clutching her handkerchief close. Charlie half expected a rebuke from Rupee, but the detective was almost approving as she watched his interrogation from the window.

"Oh, no! Heavens, no!" the landlady cried. "Mister Baker would never! What happened to Lionel—! Nothing like that! He'd never!"

Charlie and Rupee shared a long look. She didn't even appear to hate him, presently.

"Ma'am," Rupee began patiently, "we're just asking if Baker had any issues with our victim that you knew about. You never know when a man who has to leave his lodgings suddenly could use a few more coins just to leave the window unlocked, not thinking much more of it than that."

"Oh... I just don't think he would!" the landlady exclaimed. "I honestly don't know if I ever saw them interact. Possibly the odd 'hello' in the morning or evening, comings and goings, perhaps over meals in the kitchen and such, but no issues! And Mister Baker, he was such a gentle soul!"

"Do you have any forwarding details for him?" Rupee asked.

The landlady flinched.

"Yeah, we're going to need those," Rupee sighed.

Charlie kept quiet and considered the markings from the glass. A small scratch on the wallpaper here, and smear on the floor there. He was not sure he trusted the observational judgement of someone who hadn't noticed giant mirrors being moved in and out of her building — at least two nights in a row. Charlie grimaced and bit a knuckle.

He should have noticed yesterday! Perhaps not all the signs had been there, but enough of them had! The damn pieces had been right under his nose and he had failed to notice! Now they were gone!

"Oi! Detective!" Monty's voice echoed down the hallway.

They were both out the door like a shot, but Charlie let Rupee go first. He wanted to know what they'd found, and he knew his best chance of observing new information involved not getting between the two investigators who didn't like him. Monty and Florin were in the hallway and the officers were guarding Lionel's room.

"I'm all done in there, Rupee," Monty announced.

"You mind if we get him moved back to the morgue? I'll run all the important tests from there."

"Not at all," Rupee replied. "Initial findings?"

Something happened to Monty's face when Rupee asked her that. The best description Charlie could fathom was a reluctant grimace, but it was more contorted than that. She shot a long look back at Florin, who's expression was an absolute mystery, and only served to twist Monty's face further — almost like she was being forced to swallow poison.

"Honestly...?" she muttered under her breath, clearly intending her words only for Rupee but unable to keep them from being overheard by Shilling and Florin. "Initial findings suggest the same weapon and attacker as Tuppence yesterday. A copycat of the original Jack, with none of the finesse. There're marks on the ribs that suggest the heart might even have been damaged in the removal. Cheap copy, no care taken. Also, looks like our reporter friend might have been drugged first, but I'll need to run further tests to confirm that."

"Thanks, Monty," Rupee nodded. "Get him wrapped and out of here."

"Yes, Detective," Monty nodded in return and left out the front door.

That left Shilling and Florin in the hallway with Rupee, who was giving them a stern look. The warning in her eyes was of a severity Charlie thought unwarranted.

"Something bothering you, Mister Shilling?" she asked.

He shook his head.

"You know I'll break your legs if you lie to me," she warned him coolly.

"How conventionally law-abiding of you, Detective," Charlie drawled. "You don't see the irony, do you, Rupee? In all the laws you break trying to catch other people breaking laws."

She looked like she was going to hit him, which would have been worth it, and did nothing to detract from his opinion of law enforcement. However, for reasons he would never be certain of, be it morals or witnesses, she stayed her hand.

"I could see you getting pissed off in that room, Shilling," Rupee snapped at him. "What did you see?"

"Only my own inadequacies, Detective," he snapped back. "You saw what I saw: the pieces for the magic trick were being stored just down the hall from Lionel's room. I was right on top of them yesterday and I missed them! I'm furious with myself, that's all. I missed things because I was distracted by trivial nonsense." He realised what he'd said as he glimpsed Florin moving to stand at his side. Her presence made him flounder instantly. "That's not— I don't— It isn't— I'm sorry, Amy, I didn't mean— I don't... I don't mean that. Neither you nor your friends are trivial. I just... I just feel I should have cared more to protect Lionel. In hindsight, this attack was so obvious, and I just..."

"Charlie," she stopped his protests gently, placing a finger on his lips. "It's okay. I get it." She replaced her finger very briefly with her lips, and he felt like his brain shut down. "Everything's obvious in hindsight, darling.

Don't beat yourself up. Help Rupee and I work out what's going to happen next."

"I don't know what's going to happen next!" he growled, balling his hands into frustrated fists.

"Well, what kind of crime would you commit if you were going to commit a crime?" Wilson asked from by the doorway.

Everyone looked at him and he shrugged.

"Whoever's doing this is trying to set you up, right?" Bond added from beside her partner. "What do you think they'd try and set you up for next?"

"You think this is a set up?" Charlie raised an eyebrow.

"Yeah, of course," Wilson puffed out his chest. "We're not as dumb as you think we are."

As Charlie tried to wrap his brain around that, a commotion began outside. They all hurried out the doorway and along the path to see what was happening out the front. Monty was ushering the cart and handlers for Lionel's body through the cordon and it looked like she'd said something to the press, whom she was now awkwardly trying to escape as they all yelled fiercely over each other to be heard.

Then Jasper was there. Patient Jasper who had been quietly minding his own business and Susan's carriage, trying to stay away from the nastiness his charges were investigating, stepped up and placed himself like a barrier at the edge of the cordon. It was enough to cause most of the reporters to pause, if only for a moment. Jasper had mastered the same haughty air Susan had, which spoke to the deep-seated child in everyone and made you feel like you were about to be in trouble — even if you were a grown adult now and had no idea what you'd done wrong. Someone in the back had not yet been hit by the effect and bellowed an inquiry into Shilling's supposed guilt. Jasper's severity increased, and some of the reporters near him actually flinched.

"Master Shilling is many things, but he is not a killer," Jasper declared. His voice was sharp and clear. It carried. The press listened, like a class of noisy children being dressed down by their teacher. "He is a pacifist of admirable dedication, who has been alibied for both incidents — as well as many of the original crimes. The police are not investigating him, and if this is the state of our fine country's journalism, I weep for civilisation." His tone was utterly scathing, in that special way that only Jasper could be. No wonder Susan was so fond of him.

Yet, listening to him proclaim in such a fashion made Charlie's guts squirm. He wanted Jasper's assertion to be true. He needed it to be true. But it wasn't. The lie in it was like a bucket of ice water over his head. Amy had been right yesterday morning, if anyone was able to prove what had happened to Kopeck and who had done it, everything Charlie had ever worked for would start to unravel.

"Sorry…" he muttered to Rupee. "We'll get him out of here. Unless you need us for anything else, Detective?"

"You done?" Rupee cocked an eyebrow at him like she didn't quite believe it.

"For now," Charlie agreed. "I don't know what the

next step is, so I think it best I check in with some of my contacts and see if they've heard anything."

"If they have, I need you to report anything you find back to me," Rupee insisted. "Mister Shilling, I'm grateful for your help today. I'll admit, I wouldn't have found that room or the hints of the magic trick without you. The notion that there may have been witnesses to the killing is extremely promising. You did good, but if I find that you're lying to me or hiding anything, I will arrest you for obstruction of justice."

"Save your threats, Detective," Charlie sighed. "We both want this killer stopped and brought to justice. Why don't we call a truce for now? I'll share what I find, if you share what you find? Two brains and all that?"

Rupee looked reluctant. Charlie wasn't surprised. It was in the nature of law enforcement to want everything for themselves, ignoring that they always got the final collar anyway. She wanted him to hand over evidence and was reluctant to return the favour. The law was on her side too… but Lord Henry Pound was probably on Charlie's, which was how he'd become such a nuisance to police in the first place. Rupee seemed to know this because, despite her reluctance, she held out a hand to shake on it.

They shook hands, Charlie thanked the detective again for letting him have access to the crime scene, as well as Wilson and Bond for bringing him, then he pulled the side of his coat up and shielded himself and Amy as they dashed back out to join Jasper. Jasper guided them safely and dutifully into the carriage, and Charlie requested he drop them in Westminster. It was time to investigate Smoke & Arrow.

As they trundled away, curtains drawn so that no one could snap any last-minute photos of them leaving the scene, Charlie filled Amy in on everything they had found at the apartment. Present theories included Mister Baker making copies of his keys as well as unlocking the window — for a fee from any of the LOAM boys, who wouldn't? They could certainly afford to buy silence as well as favours. But why torture Lionel? Why drug him and haunt him? Why kill him? Was it really that he was a loose end? That seemed the most simple and logical answer, but if whoever was behind this was targeting Shilling, surely Lionel would have been a willing ally.

He raised all of this with Amy, who listened keenly and pondered his questions with care. There was a depth of concentration in her eyes that he found very appealing, and his own contemplation was interrupted by it. It was hard to remember sometimes that she made him smarter, that they made a good team, when just looking at her... at the way the light through the curtains framed her hair and face... could... could something... he swore he'd been having a thought... but it was gone now.

"Tanner wasn't always your enemy, you know," she mused finally. "When the papers first started writing about the little amateur sleuth who was upstaging the police... you were an underdog. Everyone was rooting for you, even Lionel Tanner."

"What's your point?" Charlie asked, ruffling his hair in frustration at the puzzle before them.

"Did he ever ask for an interview? A quote? A photo for his paper?" Amy asked.

"Of course," Charlie huffed. "All of them do."

"And you have Jasper shut the door in everyone's faces equally?" Amy smiled at him.

"Yes…" Charlie replied, aware from her tone and expression that he had done something wrong, but damned if he knew what it was.

"Tanner was a vain man," Amy reminded him, "but he wasn't always stupid. A little bit of care and the odd bit of favouritism could have made him a useful ally. He liked you, Charlie, at least to begin with. He liked the tales of your successes, before he met you as a person."

Charlie felt she was trying to tell him rather pointedly that he was rude, and he didn't need the reminder. Being honest and straightforward shouldn't be seen as rude, but so many saw it that way. Amy saw it that way. It was why she gave him that look sometimes. He just didn't have time for trivial nonsense.

"What are you saying?" he asked.

"I'm saying that buying Tanner might not have been as easy as we first thought," she replied. "We were so quick to judge and condemn him, but he might not have been as quick to agree to frame you — especially with Daddy's libel case hanging over him. Perhaps, the reason he was drugged was to hide that he didn't write the article that attacked you, and perhaps he was killed to cover that up. Also, I can't help but think that you were supposed to be the lead suspect for his death."

"You don't say?" Charlie drawled.

She gave him a look and he grimaced apologetically for being sarcastic with her.

"Charlie…" she murmured. "I think the killer knows your schedule, or at least knew you were invited to the wedding. I think they anticipated that you would skip it after the newspaper scandal. I can't help but feel the plot was to kill Sarah and frame you with Tanner's story, forcing you to drop out of the wedding and destroying your alibi for Tanner's murder — thereby framing you again."

"That makes sense, but as a plan it has been rather sloppily executed, and there must be more moving pieces to it," Charlie replied. "I mean… really, Florin, why try and invoke Harry's ghost in all of it?"

"That I'm not sure of yet," she admitted. "Charlie… you were so close to skipping the wedding… if Jane and Laura hadn't… God above, we got so lucky!"

"If Yen hadn't told me I was predictable…" Charlie mused, remembering the annoyance that had flashed through him at the accusation.

"Is that why you agreed to go?" she asked. There was a suspicious lack of judgement in her voice and he couldn't work out if it was a trap, but it wasn't in his nature to lie.

"A little," he admitted. "There were a lot of reasons to say yes, and only two reasons not to." At a slight quirk of her eyebrows he elaborated. "The attention from the papers, and the fact that I generally despise weddings. Those two meagre resistances lined up against the advantages of you, the wishes of the brides, my desire to prove Yen wrong, the seeds of investigation the wedding would allow us to sow, you again..."

"Well played..." she praised him dryly.

He smiled, glad that his attempt to suck up was working.

"We got lucky, Charlie," she repeated. "We got so lucky dodging this trap and thwarting this plot we didn't even know was being concocted. Now we just have to use that luck to find the right thread to pull. Once it unravels, we can expose the culprit."

Charlie nodded slowly. She made it sound so simple. They were on their way to investigate their next lead right now. A lead he had not disclosed to Rupee... because it would have forced him to admit that he'd stolen evidence yesterday. He'd promised to help the police. He'd even meant it. He wanted to find whoever killed Lionel and bring them to justice. No one should get away with murder.

And there it was again. That cold chill in his gut. Same as when he had heard Jasper imply he was a good person.

"Amy..." he whispered. "When... when this is over... I'm going to turn myself in for Kopeck."

"What?!" she startled.

"I have to," he defended, watching her shock and outrage. "I have to, Amy. No one should get away with murder. That includes me. I can't stand by demanding justice for others and skirting it myself. Perhaps, given the circumstances, the courts will be lenient—"

"Charlie, shut up," Amy ordered him sharply. "I

completely understand your guilt about this, but—"

"But nothing, Florin," he sighed. "I cannot hold myself to a separate standard. I just can't."

"Do you really think that going to prison will improve your behaviour or society in any way? Or is this simply to relieve your guilt?" she pressed. "Really, Charlie, you know better. I know you don't believe in incarceration as rehabilitation. You know this is a bad idea, you just feel ashamed."

"We don't have to fight about this now," Charlie muttered, looking away. "Save the argumentative energy for LOAM."

She let him have that one, but he knew they weren't done with this conversation. She wouldn't let him go without a fight. That was okay. He understood. If their positions were reversed, he would have felt the same way. It was nice that she loved him, that she didn't want him to go.

But he'd killed someone. He'd murdered another person in cold blood, and then Amy's father and two idiot police officers had helped him cover it up. It was wrong. Whatever else it was in the grand scheme of political and social machinations, it was wrong. Even if it had been done for the greater good.

They didn't speak again until Jasper pulled up outside the Smoke & Arrow. It was a tall, narrow, stone building with polished wood and brass front doors. A plaque on the front was engraved with its name. Jasper held the door for them as they climbed out, and Charlie told him not to wait. He wasn't sure where the investigation would take them after this, but it wasn't

Jasper's job to drive them all over London, and he shouldn't appropriate Susan's carriage all day. She and Rebecca might have plans of their own.

He turned to follow Florin to the club and a hand caught his arm.

"Charlie…"

He froze. Jasper never used his name. Not like that. Not unless… Charlie found himself tracing his eyes slowly up Jasper's arm, from the hand that had grabbed him up to the man's cautious gaze. He blinked, waiting for Jasper to react. Jasper didn't. His face was pinched with concern and his eyes were tight.

"Charlie…" he whispered again. "I… I could hear you… overhear you, uh, in the carriage…"

Charlie cocked his head to the side and regarded him. He wasn't sure what Jasper was getting at or what he seemed to be worried about.

"You know she's right, don't you?" Jasper whispered.

Ah. Charlie settled. That. Of course he would have a vested interest. If nothing else, he was probably obligated to tell Rebecca and Susan what he'd heard. Charlie frowned as he tried to think of a way to convince him not to.

"We understand, Charlie," Jasper pressed. "Really, we do. At least… I do. I know what it's like to have done something so hideous you don't know how to live with it, and think you deserve to be punished for it, yet know that it won't fix anything or make anything better if you are. You were the one who talked me out of that."

Charlie balked. He wasn't sure it showed externally,

but he felt his stomach do a full hundred and eighty degree flop.

"You're not a killer, Charlie…" Jasper insisted.

"Jasper…" Charlie muttered, fighting exasperation and unprepared to try and explain the situation in the middle of a street.

"You're not," Jasper insisted, his hand tightening on Charlie's arm for a moment. "Charles, a rabbit is not a predatory animal, but when backed into a corner can find its teeth and claws fatally sharp." He stepped closer, forcing Charlie to meet his eye. "Don't mistake the difference."

With those final words, he let go, looking over at a curious Florin who was watching them, and giving her a nod before he stepped up onto the carriage and began to drive away. Charlie realised he was staring after him. If he was honest with himself, he was in a bit of a stupor. He didn't know what to think. Jasper's actions and words had surprised him, even if perhaps they shouldn't have.

He shook himself from the daze and gave his mind a second to clear. Then he moved to join Florin as they headed to the front door. She gave him a look, but he shook his head dismissively. Now did not feel like the right time to disclose what Jasper had said. They could fight about it later. He could dwell on it later. Right now… right now, walking into the fox's den, it was helpful to remember that he was never the rabbit.

9

The Smoke & Arrow Club was everything Amy expected it to be. It reminded her of the club where they'd held Harry's wake, and the memory wasn't pleasant. Festive trees and decorations were abundant, yet did little to distract from reverence for a patriarchal system. If it wasn't for her name and family, there was no way they would have been admitted. The host had turned his nose up the instant he had seen Charlie, but Amy had stood her ground. Both of them had known they would be stonewalled and ridiculed at the door of this place. They had been prepared for it.

Amy drew upon every ounce of blue blood she had, even if all of it was French. She took her entitlement and confidence from both fathers, her mother's charm… and her own brilliance, quickly scouring the plaques and photos on the back wall behind the desk for something familiar.

"You know who I am," she told the host, her conviction damning as though he would dare turn away the daughter of the Lord Chief Justice, member or not. "And I'm here to see John Bullion. He's not expecting me, but he'll want to see me."

The man at the front desk paused at that. It was

barely perceptible. His declaration that the club was strictly for members only was absolute. Unwavering. Except at the mention of Bullion. Amy could see the family name on every notable item going back to the founding of the club. She knew John, and while he was generally repulsive, he was also sensible. He certainly wasn't the worst of Harry's friends.

Speaking of the worst of Harry's friends, their luck seemed to turn as the host began to soften his refusal and was cut short by a very loud and obnoxious cuss from down the hall. The vulgarity belonged to Adam Indium, quite literally one of the worst of Harry's friends and the man from his funeral who had started the gross unpleasantness that had driven her and Charlie to find any excuse to leave. He was tall and broad shouldered, with platinum blonde hair and pink cheeks. Amy did not like his face. She couldn't place her finger on it exactly. Describing his features didn't conjure any particular hideousness, not of form, and yet she found him profoundly ugly. Though that could have been his language, his complete absence of anything resembling good manners, his unbelievably repulsive sense of humour, his leering and predatory expressions, or the aggressively intimate energy he gave off that had no personal space and wouldn't permit anyone else to have any either. Overall, he was someone that Amy would have been relieved to find floating face down in the Thames, should such a blessed event ever occur.

"You have got to be shitting me!" Adam bellowed, storming down the hallway towards them. "What the hell are you doing here?! Get out!"

"Apologies, Master Indium," the host fawned. "They said they were here to see Master Bullion."

"John?" Something flashed in Adam's eyes. Amy watched as he, sure enough, came altogether too close and loomed over her like a hungry bear. "You leave him alone, whore. He's got nothing to say to you."

Amy had to grab Charlie immediately to stop him from doing something all of them would regret. He'd lunged forward, lip curled in a snarl, like he was prepared to bite Adam. Amy appreciated the sentiment, but she kissed that mouth. Not that she thought Charlie would actually have bitten someone, but she knew the instigation of violence when she saw it. Charlie was usually better than that. Still, she knew from personal experience how hard it was to resist provocation when someone insulted him. It was inevitable that he felt the same.

"I could smell the reek of your homeless rat from down the hall," Adam sneered, looking Charlie up and down as Amy held him back. "How did you two disgusting lowlifes even get through the door?"

"The usual way," Amy retorted coolly, eyeballing the offensive figure in front of her. "Doors aren't hard to navigate for most people, but Shilling and I aren't here to teach you how to use them. If John won't talk to us willingly, we can just come back with the police. There's really no need for such a display of female hysteria, Indium."

Adam cussed at her with such vulgarity that even the host drew back in alarm. The obscenity was of a suggestive nature and Amy kept a tight grip on Charlie as she stared at the man pressing in close to her.

"You wish," she countered. "But I'd never touch a pig." Adam was going a deeper shade of pink that helped support her insult. Amy drew herself up haughtily and stared him down. "Very well. We just left the company of Detective Rupee, and I'm sure the police will be curious to hear about our reception at this establishment. Discretion is obviously abhorred, so we'll let them do things their way. I can't wait to see the papers tomorrow…"

Adam was going red and pale in blotches and she could see a vein straining in his temple. It wasn't just anger. His outrage was inflamed with something else.

"Good luck with that, you meddling bitch," he spat. "The police won't touch this place. They know everyone here is of good character and properly vouched for, unlike you and your company. Anyone with half a brain knows you're lying. That ugly pet you keep's a killer! There's no way the police just let you go! I'd say they should have had you arrested, but everyone knows you're supposed to shoot mangy dogs…"

There was more than a threat in his tone as he eyed Charlie. He meant it to sound ominous. He meant it to scare them. What it actually did was harden Amy's resolve. It reminded her why they were here suffering Adam's abuse in the first place.

Because people like these men were actual killers. Because they saw other humans as less than them, as less than animals, and they didn't see anything wrong with killing them. In their twisted minds it wasn't even murder. Just pest control.

She was saved having to control her temper and respond by the sound of someone coming down the stairs behind the reception. Footsteps clopped politely at an inquisitive speed.

"Here, now, what's going on?" a voice called, and John Bullion himself appeared in the hallway.

Amy felt it bold to suggest she was pleased to see him, but it certainly didn't look immediately like it was going to hurt. John stood on the last few steps, looking over the display before him, and his icy blue eyes were instantly calculating. The solution didn't look to add up to something that pleased him. With patience and grace, he smoothed his dark hair back and cleared his throat.

"I thought I could hear you shouting, Adam," he sighed. "What seems to be the trouble?"

Adam proceeded to describe Amy and Charlie with the kind of colourful language that caused John to grimace, pinching the bridge of his nose and muttering something that, even from across the room, looked like a prayer for patience. At least the action caused Adam to stop mid-rant. John's expression was pained as he looked to them again.

"I'm so sorry, Doctor," he began, almost as though he wasn't sure what part of the fire to start putting out first. "We do have a rather strict members-only policy, not that it has ever warranted such ungentlemanly behaviour..." The look he directed at Adam was so sharp Amy was surprised no one cut themselves on it. Adam, however, did look appropriately admonished. "If it's terribly urgent, I have an office upstairs, I'm sure

I could make a brief business exception for the daughter of the Lord Chief Justice."

Adam looked like he was going to have a stroke. Amy could live with that. She wanted Charlie to come too, but this was probably going to be the best they got. If nothing else, it was good to have a measure for how forward they could be with their investigation of LOAM.

"Perhaps, Hastings, you could fetch Mister Shilling a tea while he waits?" John suggested. "No need to be inhospitable."

"Very good, Sir," the host gave a small bow.

Amy was extremely disappointed that Adam didn't explode. He looked like he was about to, and he was one of the few people on earth she really thought an unholy spray of viscera would improve.

"Adam," John addressed him, straightening the cuff of his shirt so that he didn't have to look in the man's twitchy eyes, "I need a couple of files from your father's office. He said you could pick them up for me, if you'd be so kind."

Adam looked like he was going to fight him. He looked primed and ready for an argument, but the instant John lifted his eyes, Adam balked like a kicked dog. He very suddenly became limp and wounded about the posture and face. Perhaps John's sharp gaze had finally cut him. He didn't look at them or address them again as he collected his coat and hat and left the building. Amy wasn't prepared to leave Charlie downstairs until she knew Adam was safely gone. Once he was, she gave Charlie a look and he gave her an encouraging nod.

With Adam out of the way, she really wanted John to extend his exemption to Charlie, but knew it was too much to hope for. At least it was safe to leave him here now. He looked completely nonplussed by the conditions, possibly even enthusiastic about getting tea. Amy touched his shoulder gently as she left him at the entrance and followed John upstairs.

He led her up to the third floor and she tried to take in as much as possible as they ascended. Unfortunately, they stuck to the polished mahogany staircase and the landings gave little away as to the occupation of each floor. It didn't help that half of everything was hidden behind extensive and expensive Christmas decor. The only consistencies were opulence, pride, and a reverence for tradition. It was strange, in many instances she had no quarrels with such things... but for some reason the sight of them here left a sour taste in her mouth. Perhaps Charlie's politics were starting to rub off on her. Or perhaps she didn't like it when nasty people had nice things.

John led her into his office and she noticed the room was unlabelled. Plaques adorned most walls that she had seen, vague as they were, but this room had no such distinctive markers. It was lavishly furnished, with a large, polished desk in front of the fireplace and cozy armchairs gathered around the windows. A small potted tree was decorated with white and gold ornaments and filled the office with the scent of pine. Neatly stacked bookcases lined two of the walls, interspersed with sculpted busts and ornately framed melancholic landscapes.

"I'm so sorry, Amy," John sighed, shutting the door behind them and indicating that she should make herself comfortable. "Adam is…" he sighed deeply and smoothed his hair back again. "Christ and his mothers… you know exactly how Adam is. I think the idiot might be a genuine barbarian, but his father is Lord Indium, so there's not much anyone can do."

"Mm," Amy commented, turning gently around the room as though she was admiring the art, while trying to spot anything of note. She'd heard that excuse so many times in her life, not just about Adam. When her father said things like that, she took it on board like an inconvenient tragedy. When Harry had said it, it had been a misfortune worthy of commiseration. Hearing it now, out of John's mouth, all she could think of was Charlie's stubborn and impertinent voice demanding to know 'why not?'. It didn't seem like the time and place to raise his concerns, even if it helped to make him feel closer.

John had moved to the other side of his desk and was closing over folders of paperwork he'd left open. Half of her wanted to pry, but half of her had to respect that investigation or not, John and his business were actually entitled to their privacy.

"I couldn't help but discern," John began carefully, "that you said you'd just come from the police station?"

"Not quite," Amy replied. "An active crime scene, rather. It was in consultation with the police, however."

"In consultation…?" John shot her a small smile from under his eyebrows. "Is that how you're spending your days now?"

"Don't be jealous," she quipped.

He waved away her teasing nonchalantly and flopped back in his leather desk chair.

"Not at all, Amelia. Honestly, I'm not even surprised. Good for you."

He might not have been surprised, but she was. As she considered him, lounging in his chair behind the desk, it felt strangely like it had been forever since the two of them had kept company with Harry, and yet like it had only been yesterday at the same time. The memories of evenings at the house, with the boys drinking and playing cards while she studied in the corner, came flooding back... the gentle way they'd rib her and Harry like they were a cute couple. Perhaps they had been.

John smiled at her, or perhaps at his own memories for he didn't meet her eye, instead playing with the stitching on the arm of his chair as he grinned fondly.

"It's been an age, hasn't it?" he commented, almost like he could read her mind. "But you, Amy..." and then he did look up, and his gaze struck her like a searchlight, freezing her in place. "You always wanted to help people. It's one of the things Harry loved about you. He was always raving about how wonderful you are — Saint Amelia — the perfect woman, carer of the lost and the sick. It's why you studied medicine, isn't it? You didn't have to. You never had to work a day in your life if you didn't want to. You could have just been Lord Pound's daughter, Harry's wife, you could have been anything... but you wanted to help people."

"You sound like you admire it," Amy commented, casting her eyes down to hide an annoying blush that had formed.

"I always have," John shrugged. "You've always been a remarkable woman, Amy. Harry and I thought medicine would be your calling. I'm surprised you left it."

"I didn't leave it," she snapped, her eyes flashing up with irritation. "In fact, it was offering my medical opinion on the Jack of Hearts case that got us all where we are now. In hindsight, it's no wonder Harry was so vehemently opposed to me helping Shilling catch the Jack. He knew what would happen before any of us. You all act like we did something wrong, like Harry was in the right!"

"Apologies, Amelia, I had no intention to aggravate you," John murmured, raising his hands defensively.

Now she was definitely flushed. She could feel the heat in her cheeks and across her chest. Embarrassment and irritation strained her lungs against her corset. She wanted to breathe deeply, but her attire was abruptly restricting. It was only in the sudden onset of discomfort that she noticed, and her dress wasn't the only uncomfortable thing she was dealing with. John was behaving like a gentleman, and she was the one who was rattled. She needed to pull it together, but she didn't understand why she was losing her temper in the first place.

Not until she looked back at him, really looked at him in the light coming in across the desk from the window. He reminded her of Harry. It wasn't just being in the same room as one of Harry's best friends — John reminded her of Harry. The way they dressed, the way they talked, the way they parted their hair — it was all so similar. Perhaps their differences in appearance had thrown her off at first, but when she really looked for it, it was right there. Like being in a room with him again...

After everything that had happened...

Of course she wanted to yell at him. Of course she wanted to lose her temper and beat him around the head. But this wasn't Harry. Harry was dead. She was never going to get that chance. Now, more people were dying, and unless she could get a grip and talk to John properly, they might never understand why. She took the longest, slowest, deepest breath she could, steeling herself before she spoke again.

"It's not you, John," she told him softly. "It's just... just Harry. Everyone wants to talk about him like nothing was confirmed, like things remain grey. There's nothing grey about it. The memories aren't good. He was a serial killer."

"Was he though...?" John muttered, biting at a finger.

Amy barely contained a growl, settling for a sigh as she rubbed her forehead wearily. How many damn times would she have to go through this today?!

"I just..." John muttered, his voice straining a moment as he stared fixatedly into space, as though the office door was a lost Van Gogh. "Do you ever just wonder about it, Amy? About... about him? Do you ever wake up in the middle of the night in a cold sweat and you lie in the dark and you just know… you just know it wasn't him? It just wasn't. Our Harry and that killer… they weren't the same person. Even if they shared the same body… even if they shared the same hands… it just… it just wasn't our Harry doing that. He wouldn't. Harry was a good man, Amy. He was a good person. Our Harry, the man we knew, the man we grew up with, he would never… he just wouldn't. Not our Harry."

Did she ever wake up in a cold sweat and lie in the dark? Did she ever dream her doubts… and endlessly fail to find a way to voice them? Amy felt like she was going to faint. A strange dizziness swept over her at John's words and she barely kept her balance. One hand rested delicately against the bookcase she stood by, and she was grateful for its support. As she glanced down she glimpsed something that steadied her resolve.

John tapped a knuckle on his desk, but didn't break his concentration. He still stared at the door like it was a portal to the past.

"I know what you mean, you know," he continued. "The way everyone talks about him. People talk to me like he was never real. Other people in the clubs, at the firm, in court — people who didn't know him like we did. They all talk about Harry as though he was only a killer, as though that was the real Harry and none of us knew him at all, as though no one ever really knew him and he was just this crazed, bloodthirsty maniac. But they're wrong. The Jack was the lie. That was the real lie. That wasn't Harry. We knew him. He was real. That man we knew was the real Harry… everything else just swallowed him…" John trailed off numbly, staring into the distance. He flinched a moment, as though suddenly waking, and rubbing his eyes with a pinched grip. "Sorry," he muttered. "Sorry, Amy, I didn't mean… there's just no one else to talk to about it. No one else knew him… not like us. I haven't been able to say this to anyone else, I don't mean to impose on you—"

"No," she cut off his apology. Her eyes were still on the engraved box on the shelf by her hand, but her mind was on his words. "No… it… it's fine. I… I understand…"

The craziest part was that she did. Listening to him articulate all the darkest and loneliest thoughts she hadn't let herself have over the past six months… it felt like it lit a candle in her soul. She understood what John meant, and she understood the ways it hurt. She understood not having anyone she could talk to about it. It should have been her father. She should have been able to talk to him about it, but the resolution of the Jack of Hearts case had driven a wedge between them. It wasn't fatal to their relationship, but she wasn't sure it was mendable either.

"Do you think that's why you do it?" John asked. "Your work with the police, I mean. You're still doing it because of what happened with Harry?"

"It's good work, John," she sighed. "It doesn't need to be justified."

He didn't respond to that. His eyes watched her like he was measuring her up, weighing the answer. She saw no disagreement, but it was a mystery as to what he was thinking. He looked away again before he spoke.

"I know we all fell apart after Harry's arrest," he sighed. "I know it wasn't easy for anyone… and… and no one blames you, Amy… no one—" He glanced at her and grimaced. "I know Adam and a few of the others are, well…" his grimace deepened as though his preferred descriptor was unfit to articulate in the company of a lady. Amy knew what he meant. "Well, they are the way they are… but, truly Amy, no one blames you. Not really. They're just grieving, same as us. We do all worry about you, you know. When we heard you got shot during the Kopeck case after Harry's funeral…" He met her eye with genuine concern. "I'd never dream of telling you what to do," John smiled. "If I tried, I'm sure Harry would rise from the grave to wallop me over the head, but… but we do worry about you."

"That's kind of you," Amy gave him a nod. He returned the gesture. It looked so nonchalant when he did it, as though it was an act of complete sincerity. John had always been the most tolerable of Harry's friends. Who was she kidding? John had been a frequent delight. He had his flaws, his bigotries, they all did. But he was a gentleman. Except he was a gentleman the same way that Harry had been, and for all his empathetic eloquence, she would never forget what Harry had turned out to be.

"It's funny you should mention Harry's ghost…" she murmured.

"I can't imagine how," John replied, poking at one of the reports on his desk.

"Because someone has been invoking Harry's ghost, and it's linked to the murders from the last two days," Amy told him.

"Come now, Amy," John smiled. "You're a doctor, for goodness' sake! Don't tell me you believe in ghosts."

"Not real ghosts," she agreed. "But someone has been using stage magic to 'conjure', if you will, an apparition of Harry's ghost. They were using it to terrorise the reporter who was used as a patsy for that fabrication in the paper yesterday."

John wasn't smiling anymore. Amy had watched his face as she'd revealed what she knew. She had seen the smile fall away. She had seen the strain begin to tighten his face.

"That's disgusting," John muttered.

"The blackmail, the trickery, the murders, or just besmirching Harry's name?" Amy asked.

"Do I have to choose?" John replied. He clutched his hands together and rested his elbows on the desk. "It's an ongoing investigation, correct? Why are you telling me about it?"

"Because the reporter had ties to this club," Amy divulged.

"Impossible," John shook his head. "This is an elite establishment, Amy, we don't just let anyone in — as you well know."

Amy picked up the box from the shelf beside her and held it up. It was light. The contents shifted like dried herbs and the scent that wafted from it was fragrant.

"What's in here, John?" she asked.

"Tea," he shrugged. "Amy, no common journalists

are members of this club, I can personally vouch for that."

"Just tea?" she pressed, refusing to let him throw her off as she slid the lid open to look inside. She pursed her lips. It did appear to be just tea. It certainly didn't have the smell or texture that the contents of the box Charlie had stolen from Tanner did.

"Just tea," John answered, but his voice had tightened. "You were looking for something a bit more exciting, perhaps?"

She slid the lid closed again and held the box up.

"A box of tea spiked with dried psychedelic mushrooms was found in the reporter's possession. A box exactly like this, with the Smoke & Arrow seal on it."

John frowned. He looked displeased, but not surprised. Silence hung for a moment, as though he was chewing his tongue while he deliberated his response. Finally, when he answered, it wasn't quite what Amy had expected him to say.

"It's not illegal," he announced like he was in court. Amy raised an eyebrow and his expression soured further. "We import our own tea directly, very high quality, and there are those select members who like to indulge in adding a little something extra. For some, it's citrus and bergamot, for others… they prefer something a little more earthy, with a kick."

Amy watched him carefully, but he didn't appear to be hiding anything from her. He was just being discreet in his honesty. Besides, she knew John. He wasn't the type to indulge himself. Well, maybe the citrus.

"It's not illegal," John repeated. "There is absolutely no law against it, and it keeps our more adventurous members away from the opium dens."

To that admission, she gave a small nod. It made sense. A club like this wouldn't want its members caught with their weaknesses out in public. No. They needed a way to keep their indulging private. The best way was to provide their own drugs in a safe environment, one that they controlled. Besides, opium was a drug for the common folk. They wouldn't dare.

At least, not in front of the Bullions. Not in the halls of these paradigms.

"How did the reporter end up with a box?" she asked.

John shrugged and spread his hands. "That, I cannot answer. The boxes are available to members only, but there is nothing to stop someone from ordering them and then gifting them. Nothing but quality of character," he added the last comment with a note of distaste. She met his eye with an intent to press further, but he must have seen something there because an idea lit up his face. "I tell you what, Amy, let's you and I make a deal — just between old friends."

"Oh?" she raised an eyebrow at him.

"I don't want the club mixed up in this," he stated. "I don't want the Smoke & Arrow anywhere near it. So, not here, not now, but I will get you a list of the members who have ordered or partaken in the more curious of our available substances, who would have had access to boxes of it. In return, you don't tell anyone about this."

"You're buying my silence?" she checked.

"Call it whatever you like," John shrugged. "I'm cooperating with you and we're both getting what we want without making it messy. Surely that sounds fair?"

"When and where then?" Amy asked. "If not here? I'm not waiting a week for you to help the lads cover their tracks."

"You think so little of me?" Now it was his turn to raise an eyebrow at her. "I want this over with as much as you. I'll have the list delivered to you by the end of the day. Anything to see the hideousness over."

Amy watched him as he struggled to repress his scowl, but the distaste was palpable. At least it also seemed genuine. She had no trouble believing that the last thing John wanted was his club's good name mixed up in a murder investigation or a blackmail scandal. She could trust him, for now. All that was left was to shake on it and collect Charlie.

10

Charlie still loitered by the front door of the club, drinking tea from fine china, listening to the band outside playing carols, and doing his best to only aggravate those who saw him with his mere presence and no specific actions. His notebook felt hot in his pocket, but that was just his conscience reminding him of the crime he'd committed while he waited for Hastings to bring him his tea. The plot had indeed thickened.

Amy's interrogation didn't take long, but it had given Charlie the time and opportunity he needed to steal the information he wanted. That alone made her ordeal invaluable. Even if he did have to watch her descend the stairs with Bullion escorting her like a prized object. There was tension in their postures, but familiarity. Charlie tried not to read anything into it. If it had been anyone else, he could have been logical. It was hard to be logical about Amy. He had to work at it.

Bullion wasn't rude to them as they left. Not even to Charlie. He kept a tight lid on his loathing. It barely showed in his face, only in the depths of his eyes. Shilling was impressed. Perhaps he shouldn't have been. The Bullions were known for their intense repression. This one had probably been practicing his whole life.

Shilling and Florin took their leave and exited the club, the members as grateful to have them gone as they were to have left. The sun was out and melting the snow into soot-stained sludge in the gutters. Charlie took a deep breath of Thames-scented, smoggy London air like it was a blessed relief. Despite the nearby congregation of violinists and trumpeters celebrating the impending birth of Christ, he was glad to be out of there. The tea had been good though. He was a little disappointed they hadn't tried to give him the mushroom-spiked beverage, but they were probably doing everything within their power to stop him from causing a scene at their establishment.

"I'm sorry I abandoned you downstairs," Amy apologised.

"Don't be," Charlie brushed it away, taking her hand and kissing her fingers. "It was the perfect response to the situation. Divide and conquer, if you will. I was able to gather intel downstairs while you interrogated Bullion. Besides, I think it was possibly our only chance of winning that man over. He despises me, so he will have approved of you leaving me behind to speak with him. We let him feel powerful, buttered him up, hopefully it lowered his guard — what are they doing here?!" Charlie stopped mid-thought. He and Amy had been strolling slowly away from the club, hand-in-hand, when he had caught sight of something that had stopped him in his tracks.

Across the road at a nearby café, Michael and Julian

appeared to be having breakfast at a small table in the window, basking in the sunlight. Julian didn't even look particularly hungover, although he was probably well-practiced at hiding it. Charlie marched over to them, dragging Amy along in his wake.

"Oi!" he called, striding up to the window and tapping on it. He could hear Amy trying to settle him as she squeezed his hand, but he was having none of that. This was far too suspicious. His friends grinned at him through the glass with the most infuriating expressions he could imagine. So he stomped inside to confront them.

"Good morning, Charles," Mike smiled at him over the rim of his teacup as Charlie approached the table. Charlie knew that smile. He knew it oh so well. It was pleasant, friendly, and too damn cunning for its own good. He glared at it.

"How'd it go at the club?" Julian asked around a forkful of black pudding.

Charlie eyed them both up suspiciously. Clearly they were here for him. Despite Amy's insistent pleas that they not harass his friends while they were innocently having breakfast, Charlie knew his friends. They were never innocent. They were only here to catch him mid-investigation. He watched them for any sign of what was going on. They watched him back. At least, Michael certainly did. He had a knack for outstaring Charlie. For outstaring most people, probably. Julian was pretending not to care as he ate, but every now and again would glance at Charlie's fixed attention. He also winced at the occasional loud note from the band across the street. Perhaps a touch hungover, then.

"You heard about Lionel?" Charlie deduced.

"Not before the police," Michael grimaced. "Otherwise I would have warned you. It was sitting in my in-tray when we got back from the wedding. Unfortunately, it waited until morning."

"You're only human, Mike," Julian reminded. "You can't know everything instantly all at once. Besides, Sleuth here didn't get in any trouble. The police knew he didn't bottle Tanner's heart to give to Amy for Christmas, no matter how perfect a gift it would have made."

Everyone shook their heads at him collectively. Charlie knew Julian was trying to be funny, but he had a warped sense of humour, and no one else found it remotely amusing. Julian shrugged away their disapproval like they didn't get the joke and went back to his breakfast. They did get it, all the inappropriate layers of it, it just wasn't funny. Also, Julian knew Charlie wasn't looking for a gift for Amy. Charlie had commissioned his friend to help him make her a present. It was hidden in his workshop.

"Not the time or place, my love," Skipp reprimanded gently, patting Julian's knee under the table. "We're not trying to make anything worse."

"No, you're here because Julian knows people at Smoke & Arrow and if Florin and I struck out, you wanted to make sure you were waiting in the wings to come to our rescue?" Charlie sized them up.

Julian smirked at him as he chewed. Michael just smiled as he sipped his tea.

"Something like that..." he murmured over the rim of his cup.

"Then budge up," Charlie huffed, pulling the notebook from his pocket and forcing room on the table for it. They all gathered around as he turned to the right pages and pulled his chewed pencil stub from the rings.

"Charlie, what is that?" Amy asked as she peered over his shoulder.

"Shorthand," he replied. "But I'll write it out properly and Skipp, you need to take it down."

"That's names of club members..." Michael mused thoughtfully, translating Charlie's scrawls.

"Everyone who's signed in at the desk in the last month," Charlie nodded. "It was the best I could do, given the circumstances. I only had a few minutes while Hastings was fetching tea and no one was looking. But we need to cross these names against a few lists, starting with Bronny's girls and anyone they might recognise as being a threat to Sarah Tuppence."

"Not bad, Sleuth," Julian praised, lounging proudly back in his chair.

"There's also this here that I thought was quite interesting," Charlie pointed to one name in particular.

"Baker..." Mike ruminated. "That is interesting..."

"How so?" Julian queried.

"Well, for a start, Baker was the name of the man who was Lionel's neighbour, until very recently, and a person of interest in the plot against him," Charlie informed them.

"And secondly," Michael added, "a name like 'Baker', at least if it's a real name, doesn't get you a membership at somewhere like Smoke & Arrow. They tend towards a higher value of family name. Baker's no better than Pence."

"So we assume 'Baker' isn't the gentleman's real name?" Julian checked.

"Catching on quick, Swift," Charlie nodded, as Michael patted his husband's knee. "Baker, or whomever he really is, has signed in under that identity three times in the last month that I could spot."

"I can ask around and see if anyone knows him?" Julian offered.

"Not a bad idea," Michael approved. He tilted his head slightly, regarding Amy over Charlie's shoulder. "You're awfully quiet back there, Doctor? Nothing to add?"

Charlie turned to look and guilt made his heart sink when he saw her face.

"I'm sorry I stole..." he mumbled.

"It's all right, Charlie," she sighed wearily. "It was good work. Just... be careful. If anyone finds out you took that, there will be hell to pay."

"It's just between the four of us," Charlie promised. Everyone nodded.

"John's promised me a list of names as well," Amy sighed. "A list of everyone at the club with orders of our illicit tea that Tanner ended up with. Who wants to place odds on the name 'Baker' showing up there too?"

"I'll take that bet," Julian smirked at her.

"John, huh?" Charlie echoed, hearing his own insecurity and unable to stop himself. "He's just handing that over?"

"He wants us out of his hair and this business wrapped and dealt to as much as we do," Amy shrugged. "He promised me the list by the end of the day in return for my silence regarding any involvement with their club."

"That's a good deal," Michael smiled at her.

"Aye," Julian agreed. "What did you have to threaten him with to get it?"

"Nothing," Amy replied. "He wanted to cooperate. John's entitled, I know, but he's not the worst of them by a long way."

Charlie shared a look with his friends. He did not have a high opinion of John Bullion, although he was prepared to admit the man wasn't a fool. Michael and Julian's eyes conveyed their agreement... and their concern. Amy looked set to bite back, but Charlie came to her defence.

"If you believe him, I believe you," he assured, reaching out a hand to touch her cheek gently. "You were always going to be our secret weapon in that place. I'm just glad it worked."

Her expression softened instantly when he touched her, and he couldn't stay defensive when she didn't.

"And how'd you figure that?" Julian asked.

Charlie smiled at him, still keeping his hands on Amy as she leant in close.

"Easy," Charlie grinned. "It's the way the LOAM mind works. See, all Harry's friends hated me even before the Jack, so what happened with Harry just multiplied their loathing for me. They have a tendency to fly into a blind rage the minute they see me, like what happened with Indium when we arrived. However, they all approved of Amy. Certainly, some don't anymore, but some still do, and some think that she is a poor victim taken in by my evil plot."

"Your what now?" Julian raised an eyebrow as Michael chuckled, spluttering into his tea.

"You see," Charlie continued, "in their minds, Amy is but a poor woman who doesn't have the intelligence to see me for what I really am. These idiots have taken Amy's brilliance and bestowed it on me in a manifestation of psychic power that enables me to charm and ensnare women."

Michael was desperately trying to recover from the quantity of tea he had inhaled while laughing. Julian's eyebrow looked like it was in danger of becoming a permanent fixture of disbelief.

"None of these blokes have ever actually spoken a word to you before, have they?" he asked.

"Not a one," Charlie stated proudly.

Even Amy snorted at that. They were still standing around the table, mocking the LOAM gentlemen and discussing what to do next, when a small and grubby child dashed into the café and ran up to the table. Everyone immediately recognised one of Michael's runners, even if they didn't recognise the child personally. The kid handed over a scrap of folded paper and Mike passed them a coin in return. They raced away without so much as a 'g'day' as soon as the coin was pocketed.

Michael unfolded the note and scanned it. The surprise at its contents showed instantly on his face. He looked up at Charlie and Amy from under his eyebrows.

"Hm... you two are going to have an interesting afternoon..." he commented.

Amy didn't get to find out what Michael meant until after they had been to see Bronny. They left a copy of Charlie's list with her and she promised to get back to them as soon as possible. It had been a brief visit, as Michael had warned them that Amy's father needed to see them at their earliest convenience. Lord Pound wasn't in any immediate danger, she had been assured, but he was going to need their help.

They received pointed looks from Lord Pound's staff the moment they returned to the residence, and Amy had no idea what was going on. No idea until she was shown into the library where her father was taking tea with a couple of guests. Amy was not proud of the statement of surprise she uttered when she saw them.

"Amelia! Language!" Henry scolded her.

She was ashamed of the chuckle she could hear Charlie giving off behind her. At least one of them found this scenario entertaining. She had been planning how to instigate such an occasion and now all her machinations were for nothing.

Sitting comfortably, side-by-side by some miracle, although in separate armchairs, Amy took in the self-assured and rather regal-looking pair of Marquis

Jacques Argent and his wife, Elizabeth Florin — for want of any particular name she might be using these days.

"Sorry Daddy," she muttered apologetically. "I… I just didn't expect— I'm sorry— How— What— Why are you here?!" she exclaimed, abruptly raising her hands and waving away any forthcoming replies. "Actually, please don't. I don't want to know. I don't have time for it right now. There's a new copycat killer and someone is trying to set up Charlie—"

"Oh, he's publicly 'Charlie' now, *oui?*" Argent smirked at her from across the room.

"I told you…" Elizabeth murmured smugly to him.

Amy wanted to bite. She could feel herself losing her temper, if she'd even had it to begin with. There was no particular ill-will that she bid her parents, but her relationship with them was strained to say the least. She had wanted to introduce her fathers to each other, but this wasn't how she'd imagined it. There had been no time to lay down cushioning to soften the blow for Henry. As far as she knew, both men still absolutely loathed her mother, so it was a wonder she was welcome in the house. Perhaps they were bonding over that.

It took all of Amy's strength to take a breath and respond with decorum, and part of her still flashed back to John's office like she was struggling not to release all her pent-up emotions in one destructive outburst.

"Yes, Charlie," she breathed his name like it could calm her down. "And, I'm terribly sorry to be rude, but whatever this is about will have to wait. We have much more pressing business to attend to."

"They're here to help," Charlie murmured by her shoulder.

Amy paused, her hands clasped in willed patience, and looked back over her shoulder at him. Charlie was standing with the devotion of a loyal terrier at her side. He had his hands deep in his pockets and watched the room like he was waiting for someone to try and contradict him out of spite, knowing full well that they wouldn't. His grey eyes were confident and calm, as though he had already sized up the room and calculated every occupant's intentions.

"*Oui*," Argent agreed, placing his cup and saucer gently on the table before him and folding his hands in his lap. "*Monsieur* Shilling is correct. We read the papers, Amelia. We know what's going on."

Charlie made a noticeable sound of doubt.

"All right," Elizabeth chuckled. "Fair enough, but we've spoken to Henry and he's updated us on the situation properly. We're still here to help."

"Daddy...?" Amy turned to Henry in surprise, and a little bit in confusion.

Henry didn't say anything. He stood less than a foot from her with his hands clasped before him and a neutral expression framed by his sideburns.

"You're under attack, Amelia," Argent sighed. "We all recognise it when we see it, and we won't stand for it. The three of us have our differences, I'm certain, but no one gets to come after our daughter like this."

"Well said, my Lord," Henry nodded.

Amy had a horrible vision of her two fathers

constantly nodding politely and addressing each other as 'my Lord'. She was glad she'd missed the first part of that charade. As uncomfortable as the situation was, she felt a slowly dawning appreciation for what was occurring. A strange warmth of affection blossomed in her stomach and spread up through her chest. Her lips pressed together tightly as she tried to find the words to express how she felt.

"Thank you..." was all she managed, but the sincerity was palpable.

"*Bien sûr, chérie,*" Argent replied, as he and Elizabeth both stood and embraced her. It was warm and comfortable in their arms. Strangely akin to all the fantasies she had created of her parents when she was a child. It felt the way she imagined it would. Except, now she was grown, and it wasn't the fantasy she yearned for anymore, as grateful as she was to have it.

As her parents let her go, she looked for another face in the room. The only face she wanted to see. Henry looked back at her like a mystery.

"Could I have word?" she asked for some privacy.

He gave her a polite nod and no one objected. In fact, as her father held the door to the neighbouring office invitingly for her, she could see Charlie moving to occupy the attention of her other parents. He cast her a quick look, a supportive look, as though he had read her intentions and meant to help. It was Charlie, he probably had.

They stepped into the office and Henry shut the door behind them. He looked at her curiously, questioningly, as though he really didn't understand why she had pulled him aside. There was something about his face now that was so old… so much older than he had been even just six months ago. There was so much that had happened that they hadn't talked about, and it was starting to feel like the consequences were catching up with them.

Amy intended to move towards him in a refined manner, but somehow still managed to fling herself into his arms. She buried her face in his chest and clung to him, gasping for composure. He held her tightly, his arms wrapped around her shoulders and his cheek pressed to her hair.

"I'm sorry, Daddy!" she gasped.

"You have nothing to be sorry for, darling," he murmured.

"But they just showed up unannounced!" she exclaimed softly. "And people are dying! And I'm running all over town with Charlie again! And we're in more trouble than ever! And now this ghost business—
"

"Amelia, darling," Henry pulled away to clasp her shoulders and look her in the eye, his serious face creased with more lines than she ever remembered there being. "Are you all right? If you don't want them here, just give the word. I can set them up somewhere else without any trouble."

"It's not that," she shook her head. "It's you, Dad. Are you all right? I've been making your life hell, and now this! On top of the copycat, and this nasty business bringing up Harry! I'm so sorry, Daddy. Are you okay?"

"I asked you first," Henry smiled.

Amy huffed at him. It was terribly mature on both their parts, but he was still smiling.

"I know they're technically my parents, but you're my father!" she insisted. "How you feel about this matters. And… and yes, I'm all right," she huffed. "It's not easy, but I have you and I have Charlie… I'm fine. But that's not the only thing that's important right now!"

He had the strangest smile on his face as he cupped her cheeks like she was a little girl and planted a kiss in the centre of her forehead.

"Yes, it is," he stated.

Amy wanted to retort with something flippant and indignant, but her father was still holding her cheeks and she didn't feel like she could. His smile hadn't changed. It still seemed odd, and she was trying to work out why, when she suddenly realised it was a relaxed look on his face. That was not a mood she had associated with him growing up. It wasn't something that felt like it should have been applicable in the last several months. But it was… almost like in the wake of his grief for Harry, or more likely in the experience of that grief, he had been able to let go of something Amy had never known or never understood. Something deep in her father that had left him stern, and now he had shrugged it away… there was peace beneath the pain.

"One day, darling," he murmured, letting go of her face to take gentle hold of her hands and dropping his gaze to their entwined fingers, "one day you will be a parent… and you will realise that is the only important thing. I know that. Your mother and father know that... that's why they have put aside their differences to help you. They mean well, and they have... well, a rather useful skillset between them, wouldn't you say?"

Amy nodded, even more humbled by her father's love now than she had been when Argent had first declared that they were there for her.

"So, then," Henry squeezed her fingers reassuringly, "what do you need?"

The question was like a lightbulb in her brain. When she heard it in his voice, it came with all the parental wisdom and reason she had ever known. It instilled that wisdom in her. Suddenly, she was thinking with all the clarity she felt she had been lacking since the copycat had first reared their ugly head and scared the sense out of her.

"Let's go speak to Marquis Argent and his wife," she suggested.

Henry looked suitably amused by her use of titles, and he humoured her as they left the office and returned to the others. Charlie was in the process of giving the Argents a brief summary of the case so far, although he had already made it to the investigation of Smoke & Arrow.

"So now we're mostly waiting," Charlie finished up, a note of impatience twitching the corner of his crooked lips. "Skipp, Bronny, and Yen will all let us know if anything turns up, but I'm not allowed through their personal files myself. Moreover, I don't have access to all the contacts they do. Detective Rupee also promised to keep in touch, but... we haven't disclosed our connection to Smoke & Arrow with them yet. The police have a rough description of 'Baker' and they'll be putting out a notice on a person of interest, I'm sure. Unfortunately, he is so far described as a rather bland man. Spit on any street corner in London and you'll hit three men who fit the description."

He stopped as Amy and Henry came over to join them, and looked up at her with heart-melting sincerity. His big grey eyes blinked with absolute devotion. Amy had no immunity to it. Ignoring their audience, she placed a hand on his cheek and leant over to kiss him. He had no objections, and no one commented. She was rather grateful for that, as she was certain her parents had opinions on the matter, but this answered some questions and saved some time. Certainly, no one was surprised.

"Charlie," she murmured to him, "if we're going to be discussing this for a while, could I trouble you to get us some more tea?"

"No trouble at all," he smiled, bounding to his feet.

"Amelia, that is what the help is for," Argent chided.

Charlie got that look in his eye and Amy patted his breast pocket affectionately, calming him down. He seemed to have a better hold over his emotions at the moment than she did, but she knew when looks could be deceiving. No one else tried to convince him to call for any servants, and he disappeared from the library, just as she knew he would.

Henry cocked an eyebrow at her, like he knew she'd just sent him out for a reason. Her other parents seemed to have caught on too. Perhaps it was her demeanour.

She gazed around them and they looked to her patiently. She didn't know how to begin, but fortunately she didn't have to.

"What's wrong with him?" Henry asked softly.

"Aside from the usual?" Amy smiled. "He's finally cracking. It's gotten to him. Charlie's acting like it isn't personal, like it's just another job, but the guilt is driving him crazy…" she trailed off, wondering if she dare tell them what he'd said to her in the carriage on the way to Smoke & Arrow. It didn't seem right to out the truth about Kopeck, even if Henry already knew.

"You need us to cover for him?" Elizabeth asked.

"Or protect him?" Argent added, waggling a supercilious finger at his wife.

"Both, I suppose," Amy admitted. She watched her birth parents calculating expressions before glancing at her father. Henry's eyes were understanding. "Someone is attacking Charlie," she stated. "We don't know why. Last time someone came after him like this and started killing people, it was for revenge. I won't pretend his list of enemies is short. This time they're coming after us too — they're using Harry against us and trying to copy the Jack. We need to find them and stop them and…" she paused a moment, steadying her breath, "and I'm absolutely certain Charlie can do that. He always does, but he's not good at taking care of himself and his own best interests. What I need to do, what I need your help with, is getting justice for Charlie."

"What does that look like when it's at home?" her mother asked, lifting a critical eyebrow.

"I want to clear his name, and his conscience," Amy declared.

"You don't ask much," Henry teased her gently.

"He hasn't actually been charged with any crimes though?" Argent checked. "I don't understand, clear him of what?"

Amy shot Henry a look. He met it calmly, with a note of affirmation.

"I'll see what I can do," he promised. "But you might need to talk to whatever psychiatrist his sister has him seeing."

"It's not as helpful as you might think," Amy sighed. "We've only managed to convince him to have therapy sessions with his best friend — although, I'm certain Michael will be on our side."

There were a few soft chuckles as absolutely no one was surprised by that. She sighed deeply, sharing one more look with her father before turning back to her other parents.

"You said you're here to help," she began. "And I am truly, deeply grateful. I know that you, uh, have… certain skills… and resources… perhaps that my usual acquaintances aren't so privy to…"

"Only way to catch a crook…" Argent commented, giving Elizabeth a very direct look. She smirked.

"Give us everything you have on Baker," Liz requested, "and any other persons of interest. We'll get you justice for your boy, darling."

11

People always talked about Charlie's work like it was terribly exciting. Personally, he wasn't particularly enthusiastic about chasing murderers and having buildings dropped on him. Still, it beat the part of the work no one talked about, the part the punters all forgot, which was the waiting. The putting out of feelers and waiting for the fish to bite. Waiting for the information and technical results to come in.

At least the time was easy to pass with Amy. She had insisted he stay the night and, aside from dinner with her parents, he had no complaints. Even the ones he did have, he had the sense to keep to himself.

The two of them were sitting at the breakfast table with Henry the next morning, something that had become a strangely common routine, when a message arrived. Argent and Elizabeth were just coming down to join them, when Penny dashed up with a letter and handed it to Charlie. He blinked in surprise.

"Begging your pardon, Mister Shilling," the maid murmured. "They said it was urgent."

He dismissed her apology immediately. She didn't have a thing to apologise for. It always bothered him. It wasn't enough that the aristocracy kept servants, they had to keep them submissive too. Barbaric practice. He slit the letter open and Michael's hurried scrawl greeted him.

He was on his feet in an instant. He didn't even remember standing, but he was up before he'd finished reading. Amy had her face in her hands at his side.

"God almighty," she groaned. "Who's dead now?"

"No one, I hope," Charlie replied, realising that his voice was strangely tight. "Rebecca and Susan were assaulted. Someone attacked the house last night."

Everyone was on their feet as fast as he had been. Henry was already calling for coat and carriage. Charlie was all set to be indignant about the class system again, except he was immensely grateful that everyone was pitching in to help. He wasn't sure what use they'd be when they got there. He wasn't sure what had happened, Michael's note lacked detail as he seemed to have chosen urgency instead. They had to get there to find out more, but he was certain his sisters needed him, and he was grateful for the support.

All three of Amy's parents bundled into Lord Pound's carriage with them and they moved down to Kensington with haste. It wasn't far from Mayfair, and it didn't take long, yet the seconds dragged by agonisingly. Charlie half-wished he'd run, but he knew it was foolish. It wouldn't have been faster by foot, and he couldn't bring himself to use the Underground. Not even for this.

The damage was apparent the instant they arrived. Half the streetside was cordoned off and police and emergency workers were keeping people back. Charlie was under the rope and running for the house before anyone could stop him. The front window on the second floor was smashed and there was charring around the frame. Obvious marks left from burning bottles thrown. At least the method of attack was easy to deduce. It wasn't quite as obvious as the red paint smeared beneath it. A rough hand had splattered the word 'MURDERER' in very large and obvious letters under the window. They'd had to be raised in some way… a ladder was the most logical explanation, but he'd have to get closer to see if there had been any imprints left. Perhaps they'd scaled the wall… it would have been difficult but not impossible…

"Oh God! Charlie!" Amy clutched his arm as she caught him, staring up at the damage with rather more horror than he thought was warranted. The destruction wasn't that bad. It didn't look from here as though much had caught fire, which was a miracle, given the drapes. Although, they had been open last night, and the night had been freezing, even if no new snow had fallen, and all the stored clay and experiments by the window hadn't been particularly flammable. They'd gotten very lucky.

"Charles!" a voice called over. Charlie looked over to where he had heard the familiar tones of Jasper. He was standing in the doorway of the house, where Lord Pound appeared to be using his title to gain entrance. Charlie hurried over with Amy still latched to his arm.

"Jasper! Is anyone hurt?!" Charlie demanded.

Jasper shook his head. "Not psychically, no. We got lucky. Mostly just some charred paintwork and trauma.

I think a few of your... uh... contraptions might be —"

"As long as everyone's fine, nothing else matters," Charlie insisted. "I can recreate any of my experiments, if need be."

"Charlie!" That time it was Rebecca shrieking. He'd recognise her voice half a world away. She came sprinting over and collided with him, throwing her arms around his neck. From where they stood, Charlie could glimpse through the open doorway she'd come from. Susan was in the parlour there with at least two police officers and Henry Pound. They were all talking very seriously.

"Charlie! Oh God, Charlie!" Rebecca was squeezing him like she intended to smother him. He was confident it was merely an expression of relief and affection, but it felt terribly dangerous. "It's awful!" Rebecca exclaimed. "They were screaming and wailing and things were on fire! Some witnesses say they saw a ghost!"

"It's not a ghost," Charlie gasped from the midst of her crushing embrace. "It's a man dressed in white with a collection of mirrors who seems to have it out for me. He seems to be very good at concocting elaborate plans, and very bad at doing his homework. Honestly, if they want London to believe that some vengeful spirit is out to get me, they should at least have someone watching me so that they know where to attack me."

Rebecca let him go so that she could stare incredulously at him. Amy was wearing an unsettlingly similar expression, and even Jasper was tilting a criticising eyebrow at him. It was good to have that back.

"What?" Charlie shrugged. "These murderers are sloppy! They need to do better! The fact that we haven't caught them yet when they're doing such a poor job is starting to make us look bad!"

"I'm sure Sarah and Lionel don't agree that they need to 'do better'," Amy rebuked cuttingly.

Charlie felt his lips tighten into a small frown of shame. She was right to admonish him for that. He wanted to ask why everyone was making such a big deal of this when no one had been hurt, but he understood. His own fear when he had read Michael's letter had been suffocating — worse than being squeezed by Becky. He had been scared for his sisters, until he had seen them unharmed. Everyone could safely relocate while this place was investigated and repaired. Susan had the money. Everyone would be fine. Charlie had just lost a few possessions. He didn't really care about them anyway.

But for everyone else, it had been a targeted attack against him, and who knew what would have happened if he'd been there. God above, who knew what would have happened if he'd been at home last night with Amy. The thought was enough to evoke empathy for his loved ones' concern.

"Why change the M.O.?" Jasper asked quietly, breaking the tension.

"That's a good question," Charlie sighed. "The other two were stabbed and gutted. Why change tack now...?"

"Maybe they don't want to kill you...?" Rebecca

mused hopefully. "Maybe they just want to scare you."

"Maybe," Amy politely humoured Becky, although her tone did not agree. "Or maybe they're scared of you."

"Of me?" Charlie cocked his head at her in confusion. She immediately began to smile a soft, small smile at him, like she knew something he didn't.

"What was it you said about LOAM yesterday?" she reminded. "They took all my brilliance and bestowed it on you in a form of psychic power? If the lunatic behind this really is one of those men, and they really think you set up Harry and had him killed, and tricked me into believing the cover up... if they can really believe that level of conspiracy... Charlie, they probably think you're the anti-Christ. They probably think you have horns and hooves and can compel them to do your bidding or set them on fire with a thought."

Jasper snorted at that, and Charlie had to admit that beyond the absurdity, the notion had a modicum of entertainment to it. Unfortunately, he wasn't supernatural, but neither was their killer. They just had to prove it.

"We need to go and check the front garden," Charlie announced. "It was where they launched their attack from, it will be where the evidence is."

No one tried to stop him. Indeed, Amy came with him. Any objections for fear of his safety that Rebecca and Jasper might have had were moot in the face of the substantial police presence outside. Still, as he stepped out the front door and along the front of the house, he did find his eyes were not on the scene ahead, but rather scouring the crowd at the cordon as though searching for eyes that bore ill-will over curiosity.

His own curiosity was piqued when he saw a face he recognised in the crowd. The face of a friend, who gestured towards him. Charlie touched Amy's shoulder lightly and changed direction. She followed him out and they ducked under the cordon and away from the curious onlookers. Instead, they crossed the street towards the bakery, which seemed to be booming from the excitement. It was hard to know where the line out the door ended and the nosy crowd began. A man loitered by the corner of the shop, smoking a pipe and managing to somehow appear rather inconspicuous. He wore a blue iromontsuki over hakama and directed a roguish look Charlie's way as they approached.

"You're a long way from home, Master," Charlie commented. The magician gave him a look and Charlie floundered. "I— I meant across town, not—"

"I know what you meant, Shilling," Yen smirked at him. "Don't be racist."

Charlie glowered at him and Yen's smirk widened further. It fell again as he motioned to the house with his pipe.

"I'm glad to see you're all right, lad. That's nasty business."

"We've seen worse recently," Charlie sighed. "At least no one was hurt this time. Master Yen, what are you doing in this part of town?"

"Checking on you, Shilling," Yen replied like that was the most normal thing in the world. He was still glaring at the damage to the building. "It's sloppy, isn't it? A disgrace to the art." Yen shook his head and puffed disapprovingly on his pipe. "You never like to see magic used like that. Magic is wonder and awe — we misdirect to inspire; not to hurt."

"You used to prank me all the time, Master," Charlie reminded.

"That was funny," Yen protested. "I never tried to kill you, Shilling. I never would. You're a good lad, if a bit dense sometimes."

"Is that a specific degradation or a general insult?" Charlie muttered.

Yen smirked at him again and puffed on his pipe, blowing a few smoke rings as he made them wait.

"I looked into your Pepper's Ghost," he admitted. "Funnily enough, someone acquired the pieces you'd need through a few back-alley dealings. They'd even been asking around for cheap flash paper chemicals... but in quantities that sound like they're building a firebomb..." he eyed the charred house again.

Charlie pondered that. Accelerant was only useful when applied properly. If someone had spent their energy making projectiles that were going to burn up too quickly when lit, that could explain why the damage to the house had been so mild.

"You would think that someone who practiced magic would have a better idea what they were doing..." he mused.

"Not everyone who dabbles in our art plays with fire," Yen reminded.

"Besides," Amy added softly, "you said that it would take multiple people to move the pieces of the

Pepper's Ghost trick — that implies there are multiple people involved. Perhaps there are amateurs on hand affecting the competency."

Yen pointed his pipe at Amy in fervent approval, his sharp eyes full of agreement.

"Thank God for idiots, perhaps," Charlie muttered, rubbing his brow wearily. "Does this buyer have a name that anyone knows?"

"Several," Yen puffed. "Most commonly Robert Shilling, Pierre Franc, and Thomas Baker —"

"Baker?!" Charlie interjected. Yen gave him a cunning look.

"Glad it means something," the magician grinned. "Even so, the name you might know him by even better could be 'The Great Livre'..."

Charlie and Amy both stared at him. Yen puffed on his pipe rather smugly.

"Wait... that magician who was kidnapping and blackmailing nobles?" Charlie recalled.

"The very same," Yen nodded. "You had him arrested and then skipped up north, so you missed the part where he posted bail money and then did a vanishing act. Never actually stood trial."

"If people know this, why hasn't someone turned him in?!" Amy huffed. "He's a wanted man with a grudge against Charlie!"

"Who isn't, darling?" Yen smirked at her. He turned his attention back to Shilling. "Livre had a good thing going, Charles, before you upended it. Gutting people with a knife doesn't seem his style — Livre was never particularly interested in getting his own hands dirty, hence the circus — but the magic and the targeting does imply his involvement to some extent."

"Blackmail is getting your hands dirty," Charlie replied. "It is always an ugly crime."

"So is the way the rich treat us, but they write the laws and haven't seen fit to label it a crime," Yen replied.

Charlie frowned. He couldn't fault that logic and Yen knew it too. Charlie could see in his old master's expression that Yen knew he had spoken one of Charlie's fundamental truths. But his deepest truth, the one he had broken, the one that haunted him still, was the truth his father had tried to teach him — that one bad turn does not deserve another. Vengeance was always tempting, but an eye for an eye just made the world blind. His stance with Kopeck had left a grey loophole for him to exploit... but he had killed someone, so he had no grounds on which to stand for condemning others for murder. Still, Sarah and Lionel deserved justice, and anyone else in the firing line deserved to be saved.

"Thank you for your help, Master," Charlie gave a respectful bow.

"You're welcome, lad," Yen puffed in an affectionate cloud of smoke. "However, I'm not going to find the man for you — that's your job. You asked for what I could uncover about the trick, and I did what you asked. I will not stand for magic used for murder."

"We'll fix this, Master Yen," Charlie promised.

"I'm sure you will, Shilling," Yen smiled. "Watch your lady though, there's going to be trouble there."

"With Amy?" Charlie cocked his head in surprise, turning to look at her. She wasn't there. He hadn't even noticed her step away. He double took as he realised he was alone with his friend, but Yen pointed with his pipe like he was painfully aware Charlie had missed something. It wasn't just Amy walking away that he'd missed, Yen's eyes were quite pointed on that front, and Charlie took his leave to follow after her. She was already back across the street, but his concern ebbed when he saw her reach her parents.

Marquis Argent and Lady Florin had blended themselves carefully with the crowd. They had declined to follow Pound to see Guinea, and instead seemed to be eyeing the situation from a rather cunning outside perspective. As soon as Amy reached them, they drew her in close, and Charlie could see them all conversing long before he reached them.

They stopped speaking as he approached, and he was under no illusion that their conversation alluded to him. He was under no illusion regarding the entire affair. Part of him wanted to play dumb. Sometimes Amelia Florin made him want to play dumb, to pretend he didn't know what was going on, to feign the ignorance he had genuinely suffered back when he hadn't known her so well. But it just wouldn't do. It was an insult to both of them to pretend he couldn't read her.

She was angry. She had been angry since they had arrived at Charlie's home this morning and seen his window blown in. It was a cold, venomous, deadly anger. The kind of fury that might cause one to take any new information of note about an attacker and pass it on to people who had experience hunting down and disposing of identity thieves. The kind of fury that sparked a need for vengeance.

Charlie stopped on the sidewalk a few feet back and waited. He stuck his hands in his pockets and let Amy have the space she needed to talk to her parents about what was going on without eavesdropping. But her eyes had met his, and he knew that she knew that he knew what she was doing. Neither dropped their gaze until she was ready and she beckoned him over.

"You're going to help us find Baker?" he inquired, refusing to beat around the bush.

"Consider it done," Elizabeth replied.

Argent nodded his head, but the action was more warning than agreeing. Charlie realised what he meant by the signal too late, and didn't turn until someone had already grabbed his arm.

"Sleuth!" Julian gasped breathlessly.

"Swift?" Charlie turned to him in confusion. It shouldn't have been confusing to see him here, but the state of his urgency was alarming.

"You gotta come now. Skipp's found something!" He paused long enough to take in the company and the harried air melted away. To the ladies he gave nods of familiar greeting, and Argent he ran a curious eye over. "Well now, what have we here? You must be Mister Florin?"

"Julian," Amy sighed at him, "this is Marquis Jacques Argent, yes, he is my father."

"*Bien rencontré, monsieur,*" Argent greeted him.

"*Enchanté, mon Seigneur,*" Julian replied in a way that made Amy put her hand in his face.

"No, Julian," she ordered. "What would Michael say?"

"That he needs to see you urgently," Julian replied, pulling her hand away with good humour.

"We're on our way," Charlie nodded, once he'd recovered from the slight snort he'd given watching his love and his friend interact. He hadn't been sure what he would say to Amy's parents, whether it was his place to try and stop whatever she had put into motion, but this gave him an out to postpone the concern.

Julian led them back to the bakery and up to Michael's office. They all knew the way, but it seemed right and fair that Julian chaperone them. The place was a mess, as was fast becoming its usual now that Julian was living there too. However, it seemed mostly Michael's paperwork doing the messing. The spymaster himself was standing in the middle of the room, moving between various stacks he had set up atop his bed, desk, dresser, and tables. He'd abandoned his baker's uniform for a suit, but the jacket was missing and the waistcoat unbuttoned. He was messing his hair ruefully with one hand and holding a note in the other. Julian was on him in seconds, but once his attention was diverted, he only had eyes for Shilling and Florin.

"I'm glad to see you two safe," he greeted them. "And your sisters, Sleuth."

"Thank you for the warning," Charlie replied.

"Notices after the fact seem to be my main industry," Michael sighed, untangling himself affectionately from Julian and moving to his desk. "If only we'd known sooner." He scrabbled in the paperwork, picking up some scrawled notes and handing them over. "Your Detective Rupee's been a busy woman."

"She's found something?" Charlie asked, taking the notes and trying to skim them all at once.

"She's found *the* something," Michael replied. "She's found out what happened to Harry's knife. Someone paid an officer to steal it for them, someone who had been paying said officer for a few years to overlook some petty crimes and abuses — someone who also happened to be a regular of Sarah Tuppence, briefly, before she blacklisted him."

"Baker...?" Charlie queried.

Michael shook his head slowly, his eyes absolutely damning as he answered softly.

"Adam Indium."

Charlie blinked. That should not have been as surprising as it was, but he turned to Amy to find the surprise matched. Perhaps it was not Adam's actions that were the least bit surprising, only that someone had finally found a way to catch him. Michael leant over and tapped one of the notes Charlie was holding.

"Rupee leant on the right man," he announced. "She got a confession that he stole the knife for Indium. She's got a warrant to search Smoke & Arrow for it — she's going there right now."

Charlie barely had to look Amy's way. There was no chance they were going to miss this. It was almost certainly their best connection to Baker. At least they knew who was bankrolling him — and probably who had picked Sarah as the first target.

12

Adam was a convenient and easy suspect. Amy already despised him, so hearing that he was responsible for the killings — if not the actual murderer himself — was an easy pill to swallow. It felt like the sort of thing she should have seen coming. She supposed she had. They had been investigating members of the club, after all. The motive of one of Harry's friends to resurrect his memory and retarget his victims was simple and clean, if utterly repulsive. It also further explained his outburst at seeing them yesterday, if such an explanation was required. Vulgarity of character was just as rational as panic.

The police were already at Smoke & Arrow, which made it easier to get inside than last time. All Charlie had to do was tell the officers at the door that he was here to see Rupee and they were admitted. Amy was a little suspicious of the ease, but she wasn't going to look a gift horse in the mouth.

The ease of it became apparent as the officer led them upstairs to a second-floor library where Rupee was overseeing a thorough search of the entire space. John Bullion was standing in the corner watching the ransacking like he was about to have someone sued. He began barking orders at an officer to be careful as Amy and Charlie arrived in the room. Rupee grinned at the sight of them.

"Late to the party, Mister Shilling?" she smirked. "Don't tell me I finally got one over on the boy genius?"

"Do you have the knife or Indium in custody?" Charlie asked with that genuine curiosity which felt infuriatingly pedantic to anyone on the receiving end.

Amy felt a strong swell of sympathy for Rupee and her suddenly sour expression, even if she had been trying to rub her victory in Charlie's face. Charlie seemed oblivious to her emotions, ignoring the bait she had begun with and the bitterness that followed, except to deduce that she was short on both accounts. Bullion watched them like he really wasn't sure who he wanted to see lose first.

"We have the confession," Rupee muttered, the wind going out of her sails. "There's another team searching the Indium residence as we speak. We'll find Indium and the knife. Last place he was seen was here."

"Well, he's not here now!" Bullion sneered like he was saying it for the dozenth time. "I assure you, Detective, this is wholly unnecessary. Our people are cooperating fully, and I will be having words with Justice Sterling. The men of this establishment are entitled to their privacy—"

"But not entitled to murder, Bullion," Rupee cut him off. "Our witness confessed to stealing for Indium and conducting their business here—"

"So the word of a crooked cop is enough to turn an entire well-respected establishment on its head, and justify the harassment of half the members of the House of Lords?" Bullion retorted. "No evidence, just common hearsay? Britian really is going to the dogs, isn't it?"

"John," Amy admonished him.

He didn't quite flinch as he glanced at her, but he certainly looked like he was biting his tongue. There was something in his expression… not shame, it seemed highly unlikely John could feel shame in circumstances like these, but perhaps a polite reservation of his indignation was sparked.

"Apologies, Amelia," he murmured. "It is just all terribly upsetting—" his attention was ripped from her as he saw an officer nearing one of the busts on a plinth in the corner. "Do not touch that! If you break it, you can't afford to replace it. It's worth more than you'll make in a decade!" John shook his head despairingly, even as the officer backed away. He pressed his fingers to his brow and glanced Amy's way again, the muscles around his eyes tight and strained. "It's awful, Amy. This business with Adam… is it really true? I… I just can't. I can't believe one of our own— I mean, we all miss Harry, but what an awful thing!"

"Don't act like it's news, Bullion," Charlie warned, slowly stalking around the library and watching the officers ransacking.

Amy watched as Rupee shot them all a sudden and curious look and John's eye twitched with absolute loathing.

"How could it not be news, Mister Shilling?" he grated.

"Indium and Baker were meeting at this club, during

hours you were present," Charlie replied. "Whether or not you were present for their scheming, you were aware of their alliance."

"That is unsubstantiated slander!" Bullion snapped. "I have no idea what you're talking about, and given the vindication with which you sent Lord Pound after that reporter, I'd think you'd be more careful with your own accusations."

"You going to sue me for libel, John?" Charlie looked back over his shoulder and cocked an eyebrow.

Amy wished she had a fan to cool herself. It was one of those instances where the distinction between Charlie and Shilling was apparent, and Shilling was busy being the smartest person in the room. The challenge in his gaze was razor sharp, and Bullion was all too aware. He was smart enough to know not to rise to it. That meant Shilling had realised something the rest of them hadn't.

"I don't think either of us need to take it that far," Bullion reined in his temper carefully. "But I truly have no idea what you're talking about. Adam likes to show off, he has people come by on occasion. I may have met the odd one of his friends in passing, but I have no recollection of any 'Baker'. If the police would like to attempt to validate your claims, I would be happy to grant them access to our registry and log-book."

"Thank you, Master Bullion, we will be needing that," Rupee gave him a nod.

Bullion looked like he wanted to throw Rupee and Shilling out the window. Amy could see the vein throbbing in his temple as he struggled to maintain his temper. Fortunately for John, Rupee wasn't done with Shilling, and her attention was drawn to him, which left Bullion to compose himself. Amy couldn't take her eyes off him, but she didn't know what she was looking for.

"Shilling, you tracked down Baker?" Rupee demanded. "He's associated with Indium?"

"We haven't located him," Charlie admitted. "But we followed a lead here yesterday and discovered that Baker had been frequenting the club."

"A lead you failed to disclose to me yesterday and a clue you neglected to mention?" Rupee retorted with tested patience.

"And when were you going to tell me about raiding for Adam Indium?" Charlie replied pointedly.

Amy watched her darling Charlie with concern. Everyone else in the room looked like they wanted to bite him, and he thus far seemed oblivious to it. No wonder he made enemies everywhere he went.

"A point of interest, Detective," he raised, as though there wasn't a storm of tension blossoming in the room. "Baker — specifically Thomas Baker, who is also known to go by Robert Shilling and Pierre Franc—"

"I know that name," Rupee interrupted him sharply.

"Of course you do," Shilling nodded. "Like myself, you may know him better as The Great Livre — that magician who escaped custody some weeks ago. I understand he is quite skilled at disguising himself, as well as setting up illusions, drugging people, and committing various petty crimes — especially when bankrolled by Indium."

"Now, hold on—!" John began, but fell silent,

expression stricken, at the looks Rupee and Shilling directed his way.

The two investigators eyed him up with calculating and inviting stares. Anything he had to say, they were eager to hear, but anything he had to say could be used against him to further their investigation. John stayed carefully silent.

"A private word, Detective?" Charlie asked, turning to Rupee. She nodded and led him out of the room. Amy moved to follow. There was nothing about Charlie's request that excluded her. In fact, his eyes invited her to accompany them as he turned to leave. However, a pained sigh caused her to pause a moment.

"Amy… please…" John muttered, soft enough only for her to hear as he stepped closer.

She turned back to him. He was stressed and traumatised, and her mind immediately raced back to their conversation in his office yesterday. She understood how much it had hurt him to lose Harry. To be going through it again, to be watching everything unravel in his own life around Adam… she wasn't surprised he was angry and hurt. If it had been her, she was certain she would be even more irrational. She didn't think he'd appreciate hearing that though.

Instead, she reached out gently and gave his arm a reassuring squeeze. It seemed to work. Some of the pain and tightness left his expression, and when she dropped her hand to follow Charlie, John didn't try and stop her. He didn't ask for anything else.

Charlie gave her a curious look as she joined him and Rupee on the stairs outside the library, but he didn't pry. She shook her head dismissively. It was nothing, after all.

"What's going on, Shilling?" Rupee muttered. "I imagine there's more you haven't told us."

"Keep an eye on Bullion," Charlie advised. "I know you're expending resources to find Indium, but pull enough of them that you can always keep eyes on Bullion."

"Charlie, John didn't—" Amy began, and then also fell silent at the look on his face.

"That's a bold move, kid," Rupee replied. "I'm going to need more than your gut."

Charlie seemed to ponder this. His mouth screwed up into a crooked little frown as he thought, and Amy could almost see the cogs turning in his head as he tried to find the words to explain what he had deduced.

"When we were here yesterday," he began, "Bullion sent Indium away as soon as we arrived."

"That's because Adam was behaving deplorably and causing a scene," Amy reminded.

"That is a perfectly logical reading of that situation," Charlie agreed.

"But...?" Amy grated.

"But Indium and Baker aren't working alone," Charlie replied. "As much as I enjoy watching you tear apart Bullion's library, the knife isn't here. It's not in the building. It will be with Indium, wherever he is, and he will be hiding. Someone will have warned him and gotten him and the weapon somewhere safe. It is completely plausible that Bullion sent Indium away yesterday to put a stop to the scene he was making, but it is even more likely that Bullion saw us descending on a panicking Indium and removed him from our immediate interest — possibly even to test if we were after him."

Rupee was massaging her weary brow as she listened.

"That's not a lot of hard fact to go off of, Shilling," she muttered.

"Then tell me that I'm wrong and ignore my advice," Charlie replied.

Rupee looked like she wanted to throttle him. Possibly she was thinking about how many bodies she'd have to wade through until Adam got to Charlie, and whether they were a sacrifice worth making. Finally, the detective sighed.

"I will do what I can," she muttered. "But getting a warrant to search this place after the confession was hard enough. Getting anything on Bullion will be worth someone's kneecaps."

"You can do it, Detective," Charlie told her.

Amy smiled as she watched him. There was that typical dismissal in his tone — the same one that was so irritating when he was listing oversights, but that was strangely uplifting when he was complimenting someone. His tone suggested that if anyone could do it, Rupee could, but in the exact same way he had previously told her she was wasting her time here — like such things were all rudimentary. Rupee did not look impressed, but she took the compliment without slapping him.

"Don't forget, Shilling, that this all ties back to you

somehow," she reminded wearily.

"Are you worried that I will?" he cocked his head.

"I dunno, boy genius," she retorted. "You say you don't forget things, but you forgot to inform me of your findings, and I'm wondering if — by that same forgetfulness — you're neglecting to mention who found the body of that woman the papers said you murdered? Is digging into that going to help me, or just trouble you?"

Rupee's response had a touch of leading sarcasm, but Amy barely heard the tone. Her hands flew to cover her gasp as she remembered. Charlie gave her a sharp look. Of course. She'd been so drugged after her surgery when she'd read the report it had barely stayed in her mind.

"John..." she whispered. "John Bullion was the civilian who found Kopeck's body..."

Charlie's surprise was sharp and genuine. Amy had completely forgotten she knew that... but it was another tie into the case. John may well have been the only person who saw Kopeck's body in the period after Charlie left it and before the police got to it. However, did that mean he knew things no one else did which warranted Charlie's suspicion? Or was it simply more trauma adding to the pile that was making him lose his cool?

"You didn't know that..." Rupee commented curiously, reading Charlie's face.

He shook his head slowly and she mused contemplatively at him. It must have been rather refreshing for her to bask in his ignorance for once.

"All right, Shilling. We're going to do a better job of keeping each other in the loop this time, yeah?" she requested.

"Yes, Detective," Amy got in before Charlie could stumble around a lie. "We'll keep in touch."

Rupee gave her a look like she knew Amy was covering for Charlie. They all knew he would have struggled to say the same and mean it, but Rupee wasn't going to push it. Not this time. Besides, she'd beaten them here. Catching Indium and solving the murders was within her grasp. The police didn't even need Shilling and Florin for this.

13

The sun was setting on the afternoon and the last of the light was harsh and sharp against the dark cloudbank to the west. The air was getting frosty, but festive lights and music across the city kept winter at bay. Charlie should have been out tracking down Indium and Baker… but half of London was looking for them. The police had issued a statement asking people to be on the lookout for the two of them as persons of interest. Even if he wasn't just going to be in the way during the search, everyone else would certainly be in his way.

Amy had left him to spend some time with his sisters. She would not be pleased to learn that had turned into a retrieval mission with Jasper. It didn't bother him. No one believed that, but it truly didn't. Susan wanted to pick up a few things from the house and bring them down the road to the hotel. Charlie and Jasper were happy to do it for her. Charlie because he liked keeping busy and his studio was otherwise currently off-limits, and Jasper because he believed in servitude and would cater to his Lady's every whim. Madman.

Charlie was using the excuse to collect things from the house to get into the studio. He wanted to check on

Amy's Christmas present. By all logic it should be fine, but logic didn't always win when he thought of her. The sight and scent of the studio immediately soothed him. The room was untouched and it was easy to pretend that nothing had happened from back here. The smell of clay and paint and varnish... the cold chill of the empty room...

A small curtain was strung up across some of the shelves by the sink and he moved to them first, pulling the fabric aside and peering in. The gift was wrapped in some old rags. He pulled the pieces out carefully and unwrapped them on the workbench. Mostly they were Charlie's creation, but he had enlisted Julian's help with some of the finishing touches.

They had made her a pair of ceramic bookends, heavy and solid at the base. The sculptures above had taken inspiration from both her medical career and her book, although Charlie was convinced the two were intertwined. He had allowed Julian's input, as his friend had a gift for art as well as a distinctive and different reading of Amy's book from Charlie's own interpretation.

Whatever else they were, the silver instruments with the red books, yellow flowers, and decorative greenery looked like an appropriately festive gift. Also, based on her reaction to the vase he had gifted her at her graduation, he was confident she would think them beautiful. That was the most important thing. That, and their continued safety.

He considered taking them across the road for safekeeping, and then decided he was being ridiculous.

They were safe here. The house had been attacked and the bookends had been fine. No one was going to ransack the place while it was under investigation. He wrapped the bookends safely in their respective rags and tucked them away again.

Clearly the stress was getting to him. He really needed to relax. Once the police had Indium or Baker, he was going to need his wits about him. He stood from the shelves and stretched his back out, looking around. His eyes caught his messy workstation and he wondered if he could strip down, roll up his sleeves, and get stuck in — or if he'd just get in trouble. Was the trouble worth a few minutes of throwing clay? Maybe. He was already hanging up his jacket and rolling up his cuffs.

He ducked out the back door to check on one of the buckets of porcelain he was keeping under the stairs. Susan, of course, had the nativity scene set up against the back of the house where Charlie needed to get to. The position kept the statues under the eaves and safe from the worst of the weather. Charlie was personally of the opinion that there were better things to make with clay than a bunch of large porcelain figures from a storybook.

His agnostic leanings aside, he found the life-sized statues ridiculous and impractical. As well as poorly formed. He did not know who had made them for her family, but he privately suspected they did not sculpt many humans. Or perhaps only babies. The small, glazed Christ in the manger was adequately potato-shaped for an infant. The adult figures were altogether too soft of feature for Charlie's liking.

Also, he was now having to shuffle the wise men out of the way so that he could get under the back stairs. They were not as heavy as they looked, but they were certainly unwieldy. He shoved them aside and knelt down to peek under the stairs.

The attack came so silently and suddenly he wouldn't have caught it save for the stretched shadow he felt fall over him. Mistaking it for an unbalanced statue, he whirled around to catch it, and didn't have time to get clear. A blade had been going for his throat. He startled at the sight, barely managing to knock it away. Steel dragged up his arm, tearing his sleeve and grazing his skin.

His assailant was bigger and stronger than him, clad completely in black. A balaclava obscured their face, save for blue eyes that were bloodshot with hate. They looked like a demon in the midst of the pale nativity figures. The anger only grew worse when they missed, lunging again. Charlie grabbed the attacker's wrists in a desperate effort to keep the knife off him. The two of them tussled against the stairs. Charlie braced himself against the stone, using it to keep the bigger man from knocking him down. He could feel blood dripping down his arm. He yelled out, half for help and half from the strain. Adrenaline coursed through him, but his bloodied arm was shaking. He couldn't hold it. The blade was getting closer.

Charlie kicked out, stomping his foot on the assailant's ankle. The attacker staggered. Charlie shoved their arms back, trying to get into a more advantageous position to wrest the blade away. He settled for an escape. Lunging off the stairs, he dove behind the statues, shoving them behind him as he staggered away. Every statue hit his assailant, but he didn't dare turn to look. The sound of smashing porcelain filled the air.

Charlie gasped as he tried to stagger clear of the scene. A hand snatched the back of his waistcoat. He heard his own cry as he was yanked off his feet. He fell back, grabbing for anything he could reach. The life-size Mary was swept up in his arms and he swung the statue between him and the attacker, forcing space between them. The man in black grabbed the head of the statue, one large hand stopping it dead. He swung it away, shattering it against the side of the house like a large antique vase.

Charlie scrambled on his knees. The man in black was looming over him, and he couldn't escape again. The attacker grabbed him by the front of the shirt. Charlie grabbed the baby Jesus from the manger and smashed it over the man's head. The man didn't even flinch, just thrust the knife straight at Charlie's ribs. Charlie's hands caught the man's fist. Not like this.

But he wasn't strong enough. His hands were slick with blood. The slash in his arm burned. He felt the point of the knife break his skin. He couldn't stop it. His muscles burned and strained. There was nothing he could do. The bigger man was stronger. Charlie couldn't win. This seemed like such a pathetic way to die, but he could feel the blade sinking into his chest. This was it.

Then the assailant fell back. Charlie heard a loud crack, a yell. He collapsed on his knees by the empty crib. There was nothing holding him up anymore. His hands clutched the wound in his body, trying to slow the bleeding. He looked up, dizzy and strained, into the harsh afternoon sunset. Shadows danced across his vision.

Jasper was standing there with a shovel, holding it in both hands like a weapon. The attacker staggered away. The man eyed up the two of them for only a moment, before turning and fleeing for the garden wall.

"Stop him!" Charlie cried, trying to stagger to his feet and follow.

"Charles!" Jasper ignored him, dropping the shovel to grab him.

Charlie felt his knees tremble and his steps wobble, but then Jasper had him. He felt himself collapse into the taller man's arms. Jasper scooped him up and sat him down on the stairs.

"We have to—" Charlie gasped, still trying to pursue the fleeing assailant.

"Charlie, stop it!" Jasper ordered. He pulled Charlie's hands from his body to check the damage. Jasper's face was pale and stricken. Charlie was certain it wasn't that bad... but he was also woozy and covered in blood.

And... and he couldn't stand up...

His legs didn't have the strength to hold him.

"We have to get you to a doctor," Jasper urged, reapplying pressure to the wound.

"Amy..." Charlie muttered, accepting that if he had

to have a doctor there was one he could tolerate.

He heard more than saw Jasper frown. The butler bundled him up carefully and carried him through the house. His gait was urgent and stressed. Charlie was jostled by the rush of it. Jasper never moved like that. He was always measured and calm.

He practically kicked open the front door and ran across the street. He definitely kicked at the door of the bakery in lieu of knocking. Charlie heard people startle at the sight of them.

It still wasn't that bad…

Then he heard Terry curse as the door was hauled open.

"Please help," Jasper begged. "We walked here. I don't have the carriage. He needs a doctor."

"Get him upstairs," Terry ordered.

What happened next passed in a blur for Charlie. He was carried up to Michael's room, whereupon Julian and Michael spent a great deal of effort fussing over him and sending other Pence siblings to run messages. Julian tipped a small bottle to his lips. Charlie tried to protest, but the taste was familiar and comforting, if intensely unpleasant. Everything became foggy.

It seemed like no time at all before Rebecca was there suddenly. He lay on the floor for what felt like both a long and short time, with his head in his sister's lap, while people pressed towels to his bleeding abdomen. He tried to apologise for breaking the nativity. He had smashed baby Jesus. Her reaction wasn't expected. Strange. He heard her laugh, but he felt her cry. Becky stroked his hair comfortingly as he drifted hazily in and out of consciousness. Everything hurt.

He had a vague notion that she hummed to him. For a brief moment, he surfaced from the darkness, dumbfounded once more at everyone else's panic, and realised that he wasn't a little boy that Becky was putting to bed back in their old house attached to the church. But he could hear carols. That must be the choir practicing… it must…

He remembered the way, back when he had been small, that he would squint at her when she put him to bed, and pretend that the haze of expression he saw was what his mother had looked like.

In the depths of the fog, Amy arrived. Even injured and drugged, Charlie knew her. His eyelids were heavy and everything was a blur… but he could smell her perfume. The first whiff of it was like a cleansing wash across his brain. He murmured her name and she answered. He could hear the underlying fury and terror in her voice beneath layers of forced comfort. Then her hands were on him, and he knew her touch even if he wasn't looking.

She asked what he'd had and he wanted to tell her 'nothing', but his lips were stiff and his tongue heavy. He heard Julian tell her that they'd fed him the small bottle of cough syrup she'd given him at the wedding — just to take the edge off the pain. He'd forgotten about that. That was strange… he could still taste the syrup on his tongue, sticky and bitter in the back of his throat… how had he forgotten…?

Reality hit harder as Amy began to stitch him back up. Just as he'd been getting used to the pain and the wounds had started to clot, there was a bloody doctor poking needles in the cuts. She shushed his complaints and he surrendered, letting Amy sew the wounds closed while Becky held and petted him comfortingly.

He was stitched and bandaged by the time the next knock came at the door. The pain of having his wounds cleaned and stitched had sobered him significantly. He still felt weak and sore, but that would take some time to come right. It was stupid, really. He should have been expecting the attack. It had been all but signposted. Disclosing that he had been jumped by a man who was more than likely Indium, and then only survived because Jasper had come to his rescue, was rather humiliating. Not that anyone else seemed to think so. They were all serious as the grave about the affair. Charlie could recognise vengeance in their eyes when he saw it.

He half expected the knock to be Rupee, but it was the Argents that Terry led upstairs into the crowded room Shilling had covered in blood. They eyed everyone with some surprise as they entered.

"Amelia, darling, we came as soon as we heard!" Elizabeth crossed to her daughter, placing a supportive hand on her shoulder.

"You've looked better, Shilling," Argent commented.

Charlie rolled his eyes in acknowledgement. There had probably been few times when he had looked worse.

"He's going to be all right," Rebecca sighed. "Thanks to Christ, his mothers, and your daughter." She glanced at Amy as she said it and Amy gave a weary nod of confirmation. She looked exhausted now that the adrenaline had worn off, and there was so much deep, concentrated anger behind her eyes Charlie felt guilty just looking at it. There was power behind that fury, and he knew everyone could see it. Worse, they were prepared to enable it.

"What have you found?" Amy asked her parents, the coolness with which she reined in her temper was all that kept the question from being a demand.

"Baker, actually," Elizabeth answered, although her tone was tinged with hesitation.

"There's just one petite problem..." Argent grimaced.

After everything else, Baker's death wasn't a surprise. It was almost more surprising he hadn't been found dead sooner. Given the horror of what had happened to Charlie, Amy was starting to feel like there was nothing that could surprise her anymore. She was wrong.

They were in the morgue after dark by request of her father, Lord Henry Pound, who had organised for them to inspect the body of the late magician. Amy wasn't entirely sure she recognised him, blue, lifeless, and out of makeup. Charlie did though. He was moving stiffly, and she had been loath to bring him, but he insisted.

She had all three parents with her, watching patiently, as Charlie confirmed this was indeed the magician he remembered apprehending, the same one the police had been looking for. None of that was what was surprising. No. That was all elementary. The surprising part was Monty.

Monty sat at her desk in the corner, dead-eyed and terrified. The keys to the morgue were still half hanging from her pocket and her paperwork was in a shambles. She looked petrified, and she had all but ignored Shilling. Her eyes were on Baker and they never left him. She didn't say a word as Amy conducted her own, brief, examination.

Charlie was starting to shiver.

"Charlie, sweetheart, you need to be resting," she advised.

"I'm fine," he chattered, wincing as he tensed.

Amy gave Henry a look. Her father gave an understanding nod and put a hand on Charlie's back to guide him out of the cold.

"Indium didn't do this," Charlie announced.

"I know, Charlie," Amy replied.

He met her eye. He was in so much pain, but she could see him all but oblivious to the damage he'd sustained from the attack as his mind fixated on the case. The obsessive personality always won. Still, when he looked at her, there was so much faith and trust in his eyes that it hurt. It hurt to think what would have happened if Jasper hadn't been there. The notion left her like the body on the slab, cold and numb with a gaping hole where the heart should be. Charlie didn't fight them. He trusted her to solve this as he let Henry usher him away. They paused once in the doorway. Henry turned back.

"Don't let her out of your sight," he ordered.

"Wouldn't dream of it, Pound," Elizabeth promised.

Henry's expression did not give a great deal of weight to Lady Florin's promises, but a nod from Argent settled him enough to escort Charlie away. Once they were gone, everyone else watched Amy work in silence. She didn't need the quiet to focus. It wasn't hard to see what had happened… and the stark differences from the last two bodies.

"Your freak's in bad shape…" Monty commented finally, once Henry and Charlie were long gone. "Hardly fair to go and make him uglier."

"Does being rude make you less afraid, Monty?" Amy asked damningly. She wasn't looking, but she could sense Monty flinch. She lay down her tools and removed her gloves, turning to face the cowering mortician. "How much have you helped them?"

"Excuse you?!" Monty demanded.

"Who's involved, Monty, and how much have you helped them?" Amy repeated, staring her down coolly. "Charlie won't accuse you. He thinks you're incompetent, not criminal. But you're terrified. Someone's cleaning up loose ends, and you don't want to be one of them."

"I didn't help anyone," Monty retorted. "I only ever did my job."

"Badly," Amy snapped. "And threw baseless accusations at Shilling while you were at it. You knew these murders were copycat killings and you used it as an opportunity to try and put the investigator in prison instead of turning on your friends! Well, Monty, the boys are cleaning house. Baker here stopped being useful and undoubtedly knew too much. How much do you know?"

"I know the Jack is really back," Monty muttered. "This wasn't the copycat. This was clean, efficient, expertly done. This was the Jack of Hearts."

"No," Amy shook her head. "It was another copycat. Just a better one. Think, Monty. If a group of Harry's lackies all decided to study his work, if they knew what he had done, if they wanted to continue it — there would be the ones who could do it well and the ones who were mere imitators. The police already have a confession that Adam Indium got the knife. He's been working with Baker and yourself to try and get Charlie arrested. A convoluted plan for a bunch of shmucks. But Charlie's right — you idiots couldn't come up with this yourself. Someone else organised it."

"I didn't do anything," Monty grated desperately. "I don't like Shilling, but that ain't a crime. I never framed him. I never tried to."

"Who told you to say that Tuppence was a victim of the original Jack?" Amy demanded.

"No one!" Monty protested. "I don't know about you, Doc, but aside from the Jack's victims I don't get a lot of carved up bodies missing their hearts on my table! Everyone else understands that, I don't know why you struggle with it."

"Everyone else?" Amy pressed. "You talk to a lot of people about your work?"

"Some," Monty shrugged defensively. "I'm not

disclosing anything I shouldn't."

"Anyone take a particular interest?" Amy inquired.

Monty glared at her and she knew she'd struck gold. Unfortunately, she didn't have proof. That meant she was going to have to gamble to get more. If she guessed wrong, Monty would know she didn't have enough evidence to catch anyone… but if she could get it right, if she could keep Monty spooked… maybe they had a chance.

All she had was a cold dread in her gut, an anger deeper than any she'd ever known… and Charlie's intuition. He wasn't here, but his faith in her had been absolute. He wasn't here, because someone had tried to kill him — twice. The grief she felt at the notion was like being encased in marble. He wasn't taking it personally, so she had to be angry for both of them. She needed to live up to his faith in her. She needed to do a Charlie, and right now, with his blood barely washed off her hands, she trusted his insight more than her own. She trusted his hunch.

"Did John Bullion ever take a particular interest?" she asked, her voice icy.

Monty baulked. She had a terrible poker face, and Amy wasn't surprised the boys had taken a liking to her. She would have been subservient, useful, and easy to read and manipulate. Everything they thought women should be. Amy didn't have time to fix Monty's problems. She had too many of her own. Adam hadn't killed Baker. John had. Amy turned to her parents.

"Can you get me into Smoke & Arrow?" she asked.

The two of them smirked at her, and she suddenly

knew where she'd gotten her brazen confidence from, even if she hadn't been raised with it. Not that Henry had ever been anything but supportive, but some conviction was hereditary.

"Darling, we can get you into Buckingham Palace," Elizabeth declared.

Charlie still felt weak and lightheaded. His wounds burned, but there was no time to acknowledge it. The hunt was on. Baker's death proved that they were backing their quarry into a corner. Dogs bit harder when threatened, and these ones had already done a lot of damage. The ringleader was trying to make sure that anyone who might squeal wasn't in a position to, and Shilling and Florin needed to catch them before they took anymore lives. He even had a good idea who to be watching. Unfortunately, he'd left that in the hands of the police. The state of his own body was a testament to that wisdom.

Even more unfortunately, he wasn't in a position to dodge that confrontation. As Henry led him upstairs from the morgue, back into the heated parts of the building, Rupee was striding in the other direction. Charlie braced himself for another scolding, but the Detective eyed him up with some concern.

"My Lord," she addressed Henry. "Mister Shilling, I hear you've got us another body downstairs, and that we're lucky you're not on the slab next to it?"

"Yes," Henry patted him on the shoulder, a guiding arm still about him, like he was worried Charlie was about to run off. "Our boy Charles certainly gave us quite the scare this evening."

"I'm sure you're keeping an excellent eye on him now, my Lord," Rupee flattered.

Charlie pulled a face and stimmed his coat buttons and tried to ignore them. They were going to engage in small talk and pleasantries while all the real work happened downstairs. He wished he'd never left. Their conversation gravitated to Florin examining the body in the morgue and how clever she was. Even that, a topic of which Charlie was immensely fond, he could not tolerate as inane chitchat. His arm throbbed and the wound in his chest burned, it hurt just to breathe. He rather wished Amy had given him more drugs before sending him to rest. This was not resting.

Suddenly, the door behind them was flung open and someone barged through. Charlie reacted without thinking. He lashed out and caught Monty by the arm as she shouldered by. Her body language was defensive, scared. Her face was full of disgust. She was absorbed in it, too much so to even notice who she was passing. Charlie saw it all in an instant. He registered, and he stopped her in her tracks. She whirled as he grabbed her, surprise startling her face as she realised who had her by the arm. Charlie grimaced painfully as his injuries pulled, but he only tightened his grip.

Then it got stranger. For the first time in his life, Monty didn't look at him with loathing. She was still too startled. Too... remorseful? Charlie didn't recognise the expression on her. Something in the depths of her eyes warned him. That warning was the moment everything changed.

"Where is she?" Charlie demanded.

Monty panicked, ripping her sleeve from Charlie's weakened grip and bolting. Charlie grunted with pain from trying to keep hold and staggered as she pulled him forward.

"Shilling!" Henry scolded, grabbing him gently and keeping him upright. "What on earth, man?!"

Charlie composed himself, barely, before turning in pain to Pound and Rupee. He didn't know what his expression looked like, but it must have conveyed how he felt, because it stopped all their questions dead.

"I need your help," he bid of them.

14

Trousers, Amy discovered, were surprisingly comfortable. She had not realised quite the extent of outfits her mother had packed, but she had an inkling as to why. However, she was using the disguises, so she couldn't judge. Her parents had insisted that if they were to do things the way Amy had implied she wanted them done, then compromises had to be made. One of those was her and her mother making at least a basic attempt to dress like men. It would make the first glances in their directions less alarming once they were inside.

That decision had been based on the assumption that they would not be arriving at Smoke & Arrow to the sound of screaming. Elizabeth was picking the lock on the back door when a desperate and horrified scream came from an upstairs floor. Argent went first, sword cane in both hands and ready to draw on anyone who looked like a threat.

It was late, and the building wasn't busy, but there were more lamps lit than Amy expected. More noise and people than she had anticipated. The sounds of stomping and rattling and panic echoed into the staircases from upstairs rooms. There was a small crowd up there. Everyone had heard the scream. There hadn't been a second one.

She knew where she wanted to go and who she was after, rushing from the back hall towards the stairs on the heels of her parents. Argent stopped abruptly, throwing an arm out protectively in front of the ladies as they neared the front desk.

Amy didn't have time to ask why. The front door burst open like someone had kicked it. Someone had. Rupee was leading the charge, but Amy's jaw nearly dropped when she saw her father and Charlie entering with Rupee's officers, including Wilson and Bond. Both sides froze when they saw each other, all except for Charlie who seemed to have expected this.

"You three are in trouble—" Rupee warned, pointing a damning finger at them.

"That was Indium," Charlie interrupted, barging past everyone and going for the stairs. He had his injured arm pressed tightly to his wounded body, like he was trying to hold everything together, but his legs were working just fine as he took off up the stairs.

"Charlie!" Amy despaired after him. "Rest!"

He paused just long enough to look back and eye her new attire very deliberately. It became abruptly clear she didn't have a leg to stand on. Her attempt to infiltrate a club of murderers was the real reason he was here. Adam's scream had just been the excuse everyone needed. She chased after him, only vaguely aware of her three parents yelling after her.

Rupee was ordering her officers to sweep the building. As they reached the lit rooms, the orders fast became arrests. The detective's exact words were to arrest anyone burning anything that wasn't wood or coal. Amy heard the command echo up the stairs, louder than her and Charlie's footsteps as they raced ahead. She knew where she was going, but she was surprised he did.

"The scream came from in here," Charlie announced, like he had been able to discern that from outside the building. Sometimes he really was astounding. He swerved before they reached John's office, and she was torn between hunting down Bullion and following Charlie. Her concern for Charlie won, and she followed him through the open doorway.

It was a smoking room. The fire was low in the grate and one lonely lamp illuminated the space from a desk. Charlie had stopped just inside the doorway. He was standing very carefully away from the blood. Amy didn't stop. She stepped lightly around the dark pool, still slowly seeping across the floor. It was nice not to have to worry about her skirts trailing in the muck. She reached Adam's fallen body and checked for a pulse. He was still warm and soft, unsurprising given how recent the scream had been. Seeing Harry's knife sticking out of his chest, right through his heart, she wasn't surprised to find an absence of pulse.

"Forged suicide note," Charlie commented, inspecting a lone piece of paper on a nearby desk.

"If we weren't already onto him, it would all be rather cleverly orchestrated," Amy complimented, standing up and backing away from Adam's corpse. She met Charlie's eye and knew they were of one mind.

She led him from the room, calling for Bond's attention and directing her to their discovery, before heading for John's office.

The room was empty. The lamps were on, the window let in an icy breeze, but no one was home. Everything in here was immaculate. It was no surprise. John would have done everything in his power to make sure everything was delegated. Nothing would lead back to him. Nothing untoward would have happened in this room. The absence gave her reason to pause and consider, but Charlie didn't slow. He inspected like he already had suspicions.

"Ledge, fire escape," he announced, peering out the window. "We can't be more than two minutes behind him."

Amy wanted to point out that was a lot, especially with Charlie injured, but he wasn't going to stop. If they could catch John tonight, if they could pin him to the deaths of Adam and Baker without turning it into a manhunt, that was the right thing to do.

No one stopped them as they hurried down the stairs and out of the building. Rupee's officers all knew who they were, Charlie had arrived with them, and most of them had their hands full trying to wrangle Bullion's underlings who were all being caught red-handed, even if they didn't know exactly what they had been assisting. Amy led Charlie down the alley at the side of the building where the fire escape let down. It was dark and she wished she'd brought a lantern. The lamps from the main street barely illuminated the skinny little lane that separated Smoke & Arrow from the neighbouring buildings.

Sure enough, the fire escape was grounded. Amy crouched down in the dim light. There was water on the ground. A small puddle. It had left the dirt around the cobbles muddy, and there were footprints. Not much, just enough. She could prove someone had left this way, and if they caught John, she could prove it was his shoes. Just as she turned to tell Charlie, she heard a pistol cock.

"You just can't leave anything alone, can you, Amelia?" John muttered.

"Amy!" Charlie grabbed her and pulled her back.

"Don't!" John ordered, gun raised out of the shadows.

Charlie and Amy froze, clutching at each other in the dark beneath the fire escape, both trying to place themselves in front of the other. John stepped into the half-light. It wasn't much, little more than a silhouette of grey on black. The only part that was truly lit was the gun he held on them.

"How are you not dead?" he demanded, the pistol hovering on Charlie in a way that made Amy's insides scream. "How do you keep coming back to ruin people's lives?"

"Just lucky, I s'pose," Charlie replied, clearly unable to rein in his attitude even in the face of death.

"I think that luck's run out, freak," John retorted.

"John, no!" Amy tried to push Charlie behind her. Her heart was pounding. Her body was so tense it felt like the scream she wanted to release from her lungs was bleeding out into her organs.

Bullion paused. It wasn't enough to ease her fear, but they weren't dead yet.

"How could you, Amy?" he demanded softly. "I never wanted you to get hurt. I never wanted you to get tangled in all of this — Harry loved you! He killed for you! We were trying to honour that, to get the little bastard who had him arrested! You shouldn't have been a part of it, but… but you… look at you, Amelia… you were half the problem all along… How? How could you pick him?! He's as far from Harry as you can get!"

"I want to take that as a compliment," Charlie retorted, trying to put himself in front of Amy again. "But you're only comparing two rich, white, Englishmen, so I'm mostly concerned about your lack of comprehension."

"Drop the gun, John," Amy implored, trying to stop Charlie from getting himself killed. "We've got you for Adam, don't make it worse."

"No, you don't," John disagreed, keeping the gun confidently on Shilling. "There's no court in England that will convict me. Not with the circumstantial evidence you have. I set it up far too well. Adam was always the scapegoat. It's nice to see him finally be useful for once."

"You're that certain of yourself?" Amy challenged. "You really think you didn't slip up anywhere?"

"Mistakes are for the weak," John dismissed. "For people like you and Adam. They say if you want something done right, do it yourself. So I'm finishing this."

"John, please!" Amy begged, trying to pull Charlie

back. Even injured, he was fighting to keep her from getting between him and the gun.

"I'm sorry, Amy," John sighed. "I never wanted it to come to this. But you chose the wrong man, we have to get rid of him, and nothing else has worked."

"John!" she screamed like her protests could deflect the bullet.

"Stop!" The command came harsh and final from the shadows. "Drop the gun, John."

Everyone was frozen in their place, from the power of the cadence, if nothing else. Another gun was raised, right at Bullion's head. The back door had opened in the darkness, and the speaker stepped out, pistol raised in one hand, and lantern in the other, illuminating the standoff. Amy could feel herself shaking as she watched her father join them in the alleyway. Henry's face was as grim and cold as the night he had let the police drag Harry away. His hand was steady as he aimed, and his unflinching resolve made John look like a coward as he stared him down.

"L-Lord Pound," Bullion stammered.

"Put the gun down, lad," Henry ordered softly. "Put it down."

"No, Lord Pound!" John protested urgently. "You have to understand! You of all people have to understand!"

"I do, lad," Henry assured. There was almost a note of sympathy in his voice. "I do understand, better than anyone. But killing more people, destroying Amy's life, it won't bring Harry back."

John's hand trembled. It was barely perceptible, but

Amy saw him falter.

"Even if it would…" Henry murmured, looking over John to his daughter and meeting Amy's eyes, "I would never do it. I would never trade my daughter for my son. Give it up, John. Harry was a monster, and we both knew it. We ignored the signs, not wanting to see or know, deceiving ourselves that it wasn't so bad, but it was. It's done. Don't go any further down that path."

Footsteps pounded down the street and Amy risked a glance. Her parents burst into the mouth of the alley with Wilson and Bond behind them. All of them froze as they beheld the standoff. John's face was twisting in frustration and grief.

"It's over, John," Henry told him. "You're outnumbered. Give up and come quietly."

"No!" John spat, his hand shaking on the gun he had pointed at Charlie. "Someone has to get justice for Harry — the irony that I have to go against you for it —"

"That isn't irony," Henry told him. "You want irony? I could shoot you right here, with all these witnesses, and never be found guilty. I can do that, John, actually get away with it, because the system will excuse me for who I am, and the irony, John, is that the only person I've ever met who thought that was wrong, is the man you're pointing a gun at right now."

They all waited with bated breath. John didn't lower the gun. His face was screwed up like he was in pain.

"Come on, lad," Pound encouraged. "I won't ask again. Harry wouldn't have wanted this. He wouldn't have wanted you to threaten Amy like this, not even for

Shilling."

The tremors in John's grip eased as the tension did. He finally seemed to take a breath, though his expression was still strained. Then his resolve hardened and his hand steadied.

"Yes, he would," he insisted, staring Amy in the eye as his finger tightened.

The shot was like a thunderclap in the night. Amy screamed as she grabbed Charlie. She threw her arms around him and pinned him in. It wouldn't be the first bullet she'd taken for him. Maybe death did stalk him, but she wasn't going to let it take him.

The thoughts came in a rush, falling over each other within a second. Then John's body slumped forward, collapsing onto the cobbles. Half his face was missing where the bullet had torn through his skull at close range. Henry's gun was the one smoking. He hadn't even flinched.

It was the same pistol she'd drawn on Harry at her graduation party.

Henry lowered the gun slowly, then pocketed it like nothing had happened. Amy didn't realise she was crying until he held his arm out and she finally released a stunned and wincing Charlie to collapse in her father's embrace. Then the weeping really began.

The crowd outside Smoke & Arrow was larger than Charlie thought it would be, and he was impressed with how many people Rupee had in cuffs. She'd certainly done a hard night's work. Whether she ended up with more friends than enemies for it, only time would tell.

No one had made a move on them, not even the constables who had been in the alley with them. They were back on duty like they hadn't witnessed a thing, and the rest of them stood around watching like they weren't neck deep in the situation.

Amy had regained her composure, but Charlie could tell it was fragile. He didn't like to see her like this. The problem was, deep down, he knew things were going to get worse before they got better. It was in a private moment, while Amy was being comforted by her birth parents, that Charlie approached Henry. He wasn't sure what to say, but fortunately his Lordship seemed to know.

"You're about to upset a lot of people, Charles," he warned softly.

Charlie didn't say anything. His body hurt and he just wanted to lie down. He wanted that rest that Amy had promised him. All in good time. Henry turned to look at him, his eyes grave and a deep understanding settled in them.

"We're about to upset a lot of people, I suppose," Pound added.

"It's the right thing to do," Charlie insisted.

"You're sure?" Pound checked.

"I'm certain," Charlie assured.

"Very well then," Henry sighed.

The two of them moved as one, leaving the safety of their inconspicuous group and striding over to the police carts on the other side of the road where Rupee and her people were loading up their arrests. Large flakes of snow began to drift down from the sky. Perhaps they were in for a white Christmas after all.

"Your Lordship," Wilson nodded as they came over. "Can we help you with anything, Sir?"

"Thank you, Constable," Pound gave him a polite nod. "We're turning ourselves in."

"I beg your pardon?" Bond gave them a stunned look.

"You heard me," Henry asserted. "Shilling and I are turning ourselves in for the murders of John Bullion—"

"And Lobov Kopeck," Charlie finished, holding his wrists out for ease of cuffing. "We're confessing. You can take us to jail now."

Amy did not realise what was happening until it was too late. She hadn't been looking and she hadn't been thinking. She certainly hadn't been thinking the two of them would do anything so profoundly stupid. Not until she saw an uncomfortable and reluctant Wilson and Bond handcuffing Henry and Charlie.

"What are you doing?!" she bellowed across the street. Her charge of indignation was halted as Argent grabbed her and held her back. It didn't stop her yelling at them. "Daddy?! Charlie?! What the hell do you think you're doing?! Constable, STOP!" she screamed at them, struggling against her father's grip. Suddenly, her mother was in front of her, hands on her shoulders, helping to hold her back.

"Amy, darling—" she tried calmly.

Amy screamed over both of their gentle restraints. Her outburst had gotten the attention of Rupee, who abruptly noticed who was being arrested twelve feet away from her. That did not help the situation.

There was nothing Amy could do. It was almost like it had been planned without her, and the rest of them had somehow been in on it. She had only just regained her composure and now it was gone again. Her parents did nothing but hold her back, letting her struggle and weep and protest as she watched the police load up her father and Charlie and drive them away.

"Do something!" she screamed at her mother, who was pointlessly wiping away her tears like she actually cared.

Elizabeth's green eyes welled with sympathy, but maybe that was just the gentle snow that was beginning to fall around them.

"We did," Argent told her gently, his strong arms still keeping her pinned helplessly to his body, as though they had just stopped her from doing something stupid.

"They c-can't d-do this!" Amy wept bitterly. "They saved us! T-they c-can't—"

"*Oui*, they can," Argent disagreed, kissing the top of her snow-flecked curls affectionately. He was still trying to soothe her, as though that was even possible. "You have a good father after all, Amelia. He did the right thing. Henry did what I would have done for my little girl. And he is a Lord, things will be all right."

"You don't know that!" Amy cried.

She didn't have to be paying attention to see the look her mother shot her father. Elizabeth agreed with her. They didn't know. They didn't know what was going to happen. Henry and Charlie had just confessed to murder — like complete idiots! Even if her father could endure and win the trial that would argue his self-defence... Charlie was in trouble. Charlie was in real trouble, and he would do himself no favours, and he would attempt to sabotage the legal system out of spite!

Amy stopped struggling once the wagon was out of sight. Argent didn't let her go, but he did relax his hold. She snuffled and cried pitifully and Elizabeth slid her arms around them both, holding Amy close as she sobbed.

"Mum..." she whispered miserably, "what do I do?"

"What you always do, darling," Elizabeth murmured affectionately.

"Outsmart them all," Argent elaborated.

It took a moment to click, but it felt like her tears were blocking her brain. A few more swept loose, racing down her cheeks like the snow melting against her skin. Then it hit like lightning. The miracle she needed. Something her parents had said earlier.

"Wait..." she snuffled at them, letting go to wipe her face. "Wait, e-earlier... did you... did you say Buckingham Palace...?"

15

The station was warm and dry and there were worse places to wait. The chairs were even comfortable. It was a nice place to be resting… finally resting, just like Amy had told him to. He did wish he'd gotten more painkillers from her, but otherwise it was surprisingly pleasant. It was very apparent that this was special treatment they were receiving because he was with Lord Pound. Usually, Charlie got himself booked and thrown in the pen, or at least a holding cell. This time, they had kept him and Pound together, cuffs off, and made them comfortable in an interrogation room. At least, comfortable by Charlie's standards. Henry probably thought he was getting regular treatment. Charlie didn't want to ruin the experience for him.

The two of them sat shoulder-to-shoulder on one side of the table, in the dim and windowless room, listening to the sounds beyond the door. It was unusual for two suspects to be seated together, to be interrogated together. Against protocol. Charlie did wonder if perhaps protocol had gone out the window in this case. Rupee and her people probably had their hands full with all the other nobles they'd arrested at Smoke & Arrow. The thought put a smile on Charlie's face.

"What is wrong with you, Charles?" Henry muttered.

"A lot, I'm told," Charlie smiled. "Why do you ask?"

"We've been arrested for murder and you're smiling," Henry grumbled.

Charlie did not think Pound was the right person to admit his vindicated sense of justice to, even if his Lordship was already very aware of Charlie's politics. Now did not seem the time to smugly announce the beginnings of the fall of the aristocracy.

"Well, it's over, isn't it?" he tried instead. "Isn't it nice to think that London's safe again? The copycat is gone. You've done your city a great service, Pound. Surely that's worth a smile?"

"You have a twisted sense of humour, Shilling," Henry rebuked.

"May it serve me well in prison," Charlie prayed. "You're going to get much nicer accommodation than I will. I'm going to have to survive with the common folk — can you imagine?"

"If this is a coping mechanism, Charles, we need to get you a better therapist than your local baker," Henry commented.

"Michael is a saint," Charlie huffed. "I will hear no bad word spoken of him."

Henry didn't argue that. He let silence fall and Charlie welcomed it back. Silence was golden. It didn't last, however. He wasn't sure how long they had been sitting waiting, but it certainly felt like hours, and Pound was starting to get impatient. Maybe nervous, but Charlie wasn't really sure nervousness was something proper aristocrats experienced. People like Henry Pound and Susan Guinea did not feel things like nervousness and intimidation. That was something they caused others to feel. Their unwavering sense of superiority allowed nothing else. Still, the silence and the waiting, in a space where his power could be challenged, was starting to take its toll on the Lord. He sighed deeply and his sideburns quivered.

"We may need to give this some deeper thought," he murmured.

"We're doing the right thing, Pound," Charlie assured him again.

"Are we?" Henry asked. "Is this really right? What good is it going to do? I... I can't stop thinking about Amy, Charles. What is this going to do to her? It isn't fair. It isn't right. You and I... we aren't dangerous, not to anyone who isn't trying to kill our loved ones, and Amy... Amy doesn't deserve this!"

Charlie's jaw was so tight it felt like it was wired shut. He'd been trying not to think about that, been trying to think of anything but her. Pound was right, Amy didn't deserve this, but that didn't change anything.

"You don't have to be here..." Pound murmured.

Charlie cocked his head in confusion to stare at Henry. Pound was looking down at the table, his hands clasped, and his thumbs twiddling slowly.

"I killed John. There were many witnesses, including two officers of the law, and I will be held accountable for that," Henry stated gently. "But no one saw what

happened with Kopeck. That case is closed. We could…
I could take accountability for that. If nothing else, I
could explain that I ordered you to do it. You could look
after Amy for me, Charles, and I could —"

"It doesn't work like that," Charlie cut him off. "You
can't just take on someone else's crime."

"Actually, Shilling, I can," Henry countered. "I can,
and I think I should. I did give the order, after all, and I
think this is for the best —"

"You didn't order me to do anything —" Charlie
retorted.

"I think you'll find —" Henry argued.

"Justice must be equal, otherwise it isn't justice,"
Charlie exclaimed. He could feel his breath coming in
frustrated huffs and Pound didn't start up again, but
Charlie still felt the bitter discomfort of their fight and
the confronting truths he'd been peacefully trying to
ignore. "I know you want to make things better for
Amy," he muttered. "I do too, but we cannot abuse the
system like that, even if it was made to be abused. If
society has any hope of being a moral beacon, we have
to exhibit that morality. We took lives and we must
stand trial and be judged by our peers for it — and
Pound, our peers are the common person, whatever you
might think."

Henry cast him a wry, sidelong glance. "Would you
like a soapbox, Shilling?"

"I'll save it for court," Charlie muttered, leaning back
in his chair and placing a hand on his stinging chest.

Before they could reignite their bickering, the door
opened and Wilson and Bond joined them. The

constables looked like they'd been having a good night, despite the late hour. Of course, if Charlie had had their night, booking a long list of outraged nobles who couldn't believe their entitlement had run out, he probably would have looked just as pleased as they did.

"I confess to everything!" Henry blurted before anyone else could get so much as a 'good evening' in. "I shot John Bullion, you saw me do it! I ordered Mister Shilling here to—"

"Oh, shut up, Pound!" Charlie snapped at him.

Wilson and Bond stood by the chairs on the other side of the table, files in hand, not even having had the time to sit down and join them. Their lightly smug expressions had been briefly tempered by surprise at the outburst, but they were more entertained than anything else.

"You sure no one wants a lawyer first?" Wilson asked rather pointedly.

"Or how about a cup of tea, m'Lord?" Bond offered. "It's probably been a bit of a rough night for you. Would you like a tea?"

"I would like to get this over with, thank you, as promptly as possible," Henry replied. "I have a statement—"

"Yeah, we have that—" Wilson began. Bond elbowed him rather sharply. He glanced at her in surprise and then caught on rather obviously with an added "Yes, my Lord."

Bond did not look impressed. Wilson ignored that and pulled up a chair. Charlie found, for the first time in all his dealings with them, that he had a new appreciation for the officers who so plagued his affairs. Especially for the lack of decorum Wilson showed their present company. Charlie had always though it was just him they didn't respect, but this was nice.

"Thing is," Wilson continued, lounging in his chair and scratching his hair with the end of a pencil, "we've got a few conflicting statements." He flicked open his folder but did not hold it where Charlie or Henry could see it, perusing it himself. "It says on this report that multiple witnesses saw Bond here shoot Bullion in the line of duty while he had a gun pulled on Doctor Florin and you, Mister Shilling."

"Me?!" Bond exclaimed. Wilson glanced up at her.

"You're better at the rehabilitation and mental wellness workshops," he explained.

"Fine," Bond relented, pouting.

"And I suppose the Kopeck case is very much closed…" Charlie caught on.

"Yes, very much so," Bond agreed.

"I'm confused…" Henry began, glancing between them all while he tried to catch up.

"Well, that actually makes a lot of sense, your Lordship," Wilson tapped his pencil against the report. "It says here that you've had quite the traumatic evening and that you had a small nervous episode after nearly seeing your daughter shot again. Shilling, it says you've got concussion symptoms from cranial trauma due to the attack you suffered earlier this afternoon."

"That's quite the convenient diagnosis…" Charlie commented.

"All proper," Bond defended. "We're very lucky. We

have an excellent consulting physician who helps us with our cases sometimes..."

Dread came down over Charlie's head like a bucket of ice water. Oh no. Bond moved to open the door. Charlie realised what was happening. This was bad. This was very bad. This was worse than being arrested — or at least far more dangerous. Bond opened the door and a dark silhouette was outlined against the bright lights of the corridor beyond.

Amy stepped into the room. She was absolutely dazzling in a magnificent gown that made it look like she had spent the evening at a high society gala, as opposed to helping them chase down a serial killer. Her expression, however, spoke very loudly of murder and consequences.

Charlie and Henry shared a look. Oh... oh, they were in so much trouble. Charlie could see in Henry's eyes that he also understood the gravity of the situation. They looked back and he met Amy's gaze. She was staring at him like she had negotiated for control of the legions of Hell, and she wasn't afraid to wield them. Charlie was wondering if it was too late to bargain for prison as an option.

"Amelia...?" Henry still seemed surprised to see her.

"Hello Daddy," she replied with venom in her voice.

Her tone made Charlie want to cower under the table for the rest of the conversation. It was only going to get more painful from here.

"I hear you're feeling a little under the weather, father," Amy continued, eyeing them like a deadly snake. "I'm so sorry to hear that. The police have been very understanding about this little mishap. How about we get you home to bed and I'll get you patched up?"

"Do not take that tone with me, young lady—!" Henry began, but faltered under her glare. It was quite the glare. Charlie was trying to melt into the back of his chair. Amy's eyes flicked to him.

"What?" she snapped.

"Nothing," Charlie shook his head. "Nothing, except sorry. I'm sorry, Amy."

He had only said it because he meant it, and he hadn't expected it to trigger such a reaction, but the poison seemed to drain out of her at the apology. All that was left was his Amy, desperate and imploring and heartbroken, but still his determined and resolute Amy.

"Amelia..." Henry murmured, standing as he also saw the anger melt away. Amy strode to him and embraced her father. He pulled her into his arms and held her close, just as he had in the alleyway hours before. "You didn't do anything foolish, did you?" he muttered.

"Nothing as foolish as you did," she replied.

Charlie sat at the table and tapped his fingers quietly on the desktop. Wilson and Bond were watching him. He withdrew his hands from their scrutiny, but needed a stimulus of some release, so fell to twisting his ring. It made what was coming next easier.

When Amy let go of Henry and turned to him, Charlie didn't stand. He just looked up at her. She looked down on him. He tried to express his conflicted emotions in his gaze. She had always been good at reading him. He needed her to be good at it now. She still was. There was an understanding there when she met his eye, but there was an impatience too.

"This isn't justice," he declared softly.

"Yes, it is, Charlie," she countered just as gently, perhaps even with a touch of amusement. "It's just not conventional. To be honest, I'm surprised to find you against unconventional justice. I can't help but feel that if this were anyone else in your position, you would be extremely supportive of it."

Charlie frowned at that. That… was an annoyingly good point. She stepped closer. Her fingers came to rest under his chin, tilting his head to look at her. He didn't resist. He liked looking at her, even if it slowed his thought process.

"Think about it this way," she began, "what actual good were you hoping to achieve, save an alleviation of your own guilt?"

Charlie's frown deepened. He was trying to find the words to describe it, but the more frustrated his expression became, the more hers softened, and that made thinking difficult.

"It's about equality," he tried to explain. "We have to hold ourselves accountable to the same standard we hold everyone else. We deserve to be judged by the public. We are not above the people."

"No one thinks you are, darling," Amy told him. "And I assure you, they are judging you."

Wilson and Bond nodded in agreement. Charlie wasn't sure it helped. Perhaps a little bit, but not enough. He shook his head wearily.

"I can't, Amy," he pleaded. "I'm sorry, I just can't."

"I thought you might say that," she nodded like she'd been expecting it.

Wilson pulled two pieces of paper from his file and laid them on the table. They were extremely ornate and impressive. Bond gave a delighted little squeal. Charlie stared with growing horror.

"What. Is. That?" he demanded.

"Those are official pardons for the two of you from Her Majesty the Queen, pardoning you for any crimes committed during the resolution of the Jack of Hearts case, the Kopeck case, and the copycat case," Amy told them. "You are hereby absolved of any wrongdoing that was committed during those periods in the name of restoring the peace. Merry Christmas, my love."

Charlie felt like he'd been stabbed again.

"The Queen?!" Henry exclaimed. "Victoria?!"

"No, Daddy, the Queen of France," Amy drawled sarcastically.

He looked like he was going to scold her for her tone again, but her scathing expression was once again more powerful than his own and he let her have that one. In hindsight, it had been a stupid question.

She turned her attention back to Charlie, who was still staring at the table like she'd dropped a mutilated corpse on it.

"You should have taken the out, my love," she said. "Now you are the definition of aristocratic special treatment. Her Majesty sends her best. Apparently you do excellent work for the Empire."

He turned to look up at her again very slowly. Displeased did not begin to cover it. It was, without any competition, the worst Christmas present he had ever received.

"Thanks. I hate it," he muttered.

Amy leant down to kiss his head and he didn't stop her. He did not return the affection. He was going to need a minute. And a bath. And some whiskey. Who was he kidding? This was the kind of gold embossed filth that would never come back off. He wanted to stand up and puke all over the paper, but he wasn't sure he had it in him. Everything hurt too much and he was too tired. He huffed very angrily.

"I got outplayed by two halfwits and the most brilliant woman I've ever met..." he muttered.

"That's very kind of you, darling, but it was mostly the halfwits," Amy smiled, shooting a cheeky look at Wilson and Bond. "Turns out they may have more than half a wit."

The officers looked altogether too smug about that. Charlie gave another deep sigh. He had tried to fall on his sword and discovered that not only was there no sword to fall on, but that the cobbles beneath were only hard enough to cause embarrassing bruises to one's ego. Amy was still stroking his hair.

"Charlie..." Amy bid him softly, "how much do you have to sacrifice, and how hard do you have to try to be a good man, before you accept that you might actually be one?"

That got his attention. He looked up at her and she bid him to stand. His body was stiff and sore, but he didn't have it in him to refuse her that. He stood and slipped his arms around her waist as she embraced him.

"I love you, Charlie," she whispered, kissing his cheek. "I love you so much, and I understand. I understand that being as brilliant as you are means sometimes you have to be frighteningly imbecilic to balance it, but that's why you have me. Your heart was in the right place, but you did something stupid. I've fixed it. I already won, darling. Let me have this. You can call it my Christmas present."

He nodded, squeezing her gently. He already had a present for her, but he wasn't going to tell her that, even if this was going to be his. He had a horrible feeling that he'd earnt it. They stood in each other's arms for a moment, safe and warm. She was, he had come to realise on a daily basis, quite brilliant and he had never really stood a chance. All things considered, perhaps that wasn't so bad. When he left her embrace, it was slow and reluctant.

"What now, then?" he asked.

"Would you like a smiley stamp on your statements?" Wilson offered. "Bond makes them herself."

"I use potatoes," Bond admitted bashfully.

Charlie stared at them a moment too long and knew with horrible certainty that the world was still as insane now as it had been when he'd entered the police station. He turned to Amy.

"Please take me home," he requested.

Amy put a loving arm around him and started to walk him from the room. Henry was watching them with a strangely affectionate and proud expression.

"Don't," Charlie warned him.

"That's 'Don't, my Lord'," Henry corrected.

"Don't," Charlie protested louder.

Pound looked like he was going to laugh, but Amy gave him a gentle glance that requested they don't tease her little sleuth right now, and Henry left it at a smile. He followed in their wake as the constables saw them out. The station was bright and loud with the aftermath of the night's arrests. They passed it all as though they weren't involved and exited into the dark and cold night.

The snow was falling thick now and had settled into a soft white blanket across the ground. It was marred by the great many tracks leading to and from the police station. They were having a busy night. Pine and holly framed the building as though it were all a joyous affair, and the reflections of the streetlamps made it look like a painting. Bells were ringing from the church down the street. At least it was over.

Charlie pulled his coat tighter and winced as the cold hit his wounds. Amy huddled with him as Pound organised a carriage home.

"What about tomorrow?" Charlie muttered, watching the snow dance around them. "What about the papers and the fallout? What about—?"

Amy silenced him with a kiss, and he forgot what he'd been about to protest. A couple of light flakes of snow tickled his cheeks, as soft as her lashes. She drew her lips from his, smiling at him in the spotlight of the streetlamps, and straightened the lapels of his tattered coat.

"Tomorrow, you're going to rest," she murmured.

"And possibly for a few more days after that, if I can bully you into it. Next week, we're going to have our first Christmas together, and I have absolute confidence your sisters will force you to behave for it. After that, you're going to do what you do best. You're going to pick up new cases. You're going to help people. And I'm going to help you."

Charlie blinked at that. She made it sound awfully good. He gently slipped a hand into hers and squeezed it. She returned the gesture, turning to stand at his side as Pound signalled them to join him across the street, and rested her head against his.

"Who knows," she pondered, as they strolled gently over the road together, holding hands in the snow, "maybe next year Florence Pound will write another book about you."

Charlie rolled his eyes. Amy laughed. God, it was a beautiful laugh. It complimented the last gentle ringing of the bells in the air. She was right. Tomorrow he would rest, and everything after that could be worked out later. For now, all he needed was to get home, maybe have her check his stitches, and then collapse in bed, preferably with her at his side to make sure he stayed warm overnight. It sounded like a plan.

Thus concludes *A Cold & Bitter Revenge* Book Five of the *Shilling & Florin Mysteries*. The story continues in
BOOK SIX:
THE PEN & THE BLADE

Did you enjoy this book?

Please consider leaving a review for it on Amazon or Goodreads. Every positive review allows me to spend more time writing books for you to enjoy!

katehaleyauthor/amazon

OTHER BOOKS BY KATE HALEY

Welcome to the Inbetween

The Light After Earth

Like the Heroes of Old

Shilling & Florin Mysteries

1. The Jack of Hearts Murders

2. The Thief & the Marquis

3. A Dalliance with Grief

4. The Case of Silver & Sovereign

5. A Cold & Bitter Revenge

6. The Pen & the Blade

7. Blood & Bells

8. Tarnished Silver

The War of the North Saga

Footsteps into the Unfamiliar (short story collection)

1. Steel & Stone

2. Magic in the Marshes

3. Forest of Ghosts

4. Women of the Woods

5. Spirit & Sand

6. The Prince and the Witch

7. Gods & Dragons

The Vincent Temple Trilogy (+ Prequel)

Path of Dreaming Souls (Prequel)

1. Gateway to Dark Stars

2. Tomb of Endless Night

3. Fortress of the Shadow Reich

ABOUT THE AUTHOR

Kate Haley is a speculative fiction author who works predominantly in fantasy and horror.

While currently content to fill their days with writing and table-top RPGs, their grander plans involve world domination. Something akin to the tyranny of the greatest city atop the Disc would be an acceptable standard. They believe a super-villainous overlord would be an upgrade, given that our current villains lack style and imagination.

After all, super-villainy requires Presentation.

If you like their references, consider visiting their website www.katehaleyauthor.com for short fictions and merchandise, and join the mailing list for early access and exclusive cool stuff.

You can also get in touch through the website regarding their work, your position in future slave armies, or a general interest in all things nerdy and wonderful.